BROKEN WHEELS

A DI FRANK MILLER NOVEL

JOHN CARSON

DI FRANK MILLER SERIES

Crash Point
Silent Marker
Rain Town
Watch Me Bleed
Broken Wheels
Sudden Death
Under the Knife
Trial and Error
Warning Sign
Cut Throat
Blood from a Stone
Time of Death

Frank Miller Crime Series – Books 1-3 – Box set

MAX DOYLE SERIES

SCOTT MARSHALL SERIES

Old Habits

BROKEN WHEELS

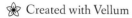 Created with Vellum

DEDICATION

For Jimmy Patterson, one of the funniest men I have ever worked with. He was a small man with a huge sense of humour. I miss working with you buddy.

PROLOGUE

The turnout for the funeral is big. She had been popular, and it shows. I'm standing near the front, close to the family but not too close.

It's autumn, halfway between summer and winter, the time of year in Scotland where the weather can swing either way, warm or cold. Today it's warm, with a light wind. They're dressed in the traditional black, some of them in long overcoats, not taking a chance. Like me.

The minister gives the usual eulogy, describing how good she was in life, although nobody doubts just how much of it is made up.

I hate them all. I'd put more than one of them in the grave with her, if I could. I keep those thoughts to myself, blending into the background. I keep my head slightly bowed. Not making eye contact with anybody.

The minister rattles on and his words float away in the wind. Finally, he finishes and those who came in the funeral cars parade back to them, while the others make their way back to the road where their own cars wait.

I'm straggling behind, just another anonymous mourner. I watch her ahead, interacting with other members of the family and friends of the deceased. I'm a nobody. For now.

'You're not crying, I hope,' I say to the man beside me, feeling repulsed.

Long hair sniffs and wipes his hand over his cheek. 'I just miss my own folks, that's all.'

Our voices are low, unable to be heard above the wind that's kicking through the trees.

'Pull yourself together for God's sake. You didn't even know the woman.'

'Why did you make me come here then?'

'It's about showing respect for a dead person.'

'Why aren't you at her side?' He nods to the woman up ahead.

'They don't know about me. Yet.'

'Won't they be overjoyed when they learn the truth about you?' He says it with a sneer, and I look around to see if anybody heard him. Nobody's paying him any attention.

'Shut up. She could do a lot worse.' I look at him. 'She could be going out with you.'

'At least I would make her happy.'

I look at him. 'Do you want to join her down there?'

He doesn't reply.

'I didn't think so.'

I'm the only one smiling. Inwardly of course. I don't want them to think I'm some kind of mutant.

I'm smiling at the memory of the old woman at the top of her stairs, at the look on her face as she realises what I've done. Forensics are too good nowadays, so pushing her wasn't an option. They would calculate her weight, and her trajectory and figure out that it would have taken a push for her head to hit x-step at y-speed, therefore the result was z. Murder.

No, it had to be a trip. Just a subtle slide of my foot in front of hers. Luckily, her toilet was at the top of the stairs. As soon as I heard her moving past the bathroom door, I was out like a flash and stuck my foot out.

The trajectory would be measured and they would see that her own weight carried her down. All I had to do was wait for the screams and then rush out, pulling my loosened belt tight – as if I'd been on the lav – and ask what was going on, shout and scream for somebody to call an ambulance!

Jesus, I almost laugh when I replay the scene in my head, and how easy it had all been.

We finally reach the roadway where the cars are.

'When we're at the funeral tea, be on your best behaviour,' I say.

'You act as if I embarrass you.'

'So, what's your point?' We get into my car and I

3

turn up the heat. 'What will they think when they see the car I'm driving?' I ask him.

'That you're a pretentious prick?'

I ignore him and laugh aloud. Smile and say one word as we pull away. 'Showtime!'

ONE

In death, at least the girl was at peace. From the scars showing on her semi-naked body, she'd had a hard life, and it hadn't been a long one.

DI Frank Miller tried to shift the image of her pale, white body from his mind but couldn't.

The cold December wind was unhindered in its progress as it shot in from the North Sea, across Portobello beach, where the Edinburgh residents would come in droves during the summer. Then, the sun would be out, the funfair would be open, and the arcades would be full of teenagers.

Now, it was a deserted wasteland, inhabited by dog walkers and joggers. The overnight snowfall had been light but more inches were forecast for later that day. He stepped out of the forensics tent with the others while the police photographer went to work.

'Jesus, poor girl,' Steffi Walker said, coming to

stand beside Miller. She'd only been with the team for a couple of months but was proving to be a great asset. As was Angie Rivers, their transplant from Aberdeen. She was walking across the snow-covered beach with Superintendent Percy Purcell, the pair looking like a couple of union conspirators.

Detective Sergeant Andy Watt was blowing into his hands as he came across to Miller with Kim Smith.

'Where's your gloves?' Purcell asked.

'I forgot them.'

'You're like a wee laddie,' Miller said as he stopped in front of the group.

'And you nag just like my ex-wife. Except she was better looking.'

'What do we have here?' Purcell asked.

'A young girl, mid-teens to early-twenties. She was stabbed through the left eye with a slim knife. We don't know if that was the cause of death yet.'

'How do you know it was a slim knife, sir?' Angie asked.

'It's still sticking out of her eye.'

'Oh.'

Miller shivered in his overcoat and pulled his woolly hat down farther round his ears. The only people on the beach this morning were police officers and a pathologist.

A few onlookers were wondering what was going on as they were kept at bay on the promenade by uniformed officers

Inside the forensic tent was one of the pathologists from Edinburgh City Mortuary, Kate Murphy.

Kate had been in Edinburgh for six months, a transplant from London. Her North London accent fought with the wind as she poked her head out of the tent. 'DI Miller? You can come back in. Bring your friends.'

They all trooped into the tent, getting a brief respite from the biting wind. 'We need to get you a propane gas heater for in here,' he said, as the flap fell back down behind him.

He looked at the girl's body. She had been moved by Kate and put back pretty much in the same place. Her face had the pallor only the dead carry and her left eye looked as if it had been destroyed. Snow had partially covered her body and she might have lain on the beach until the sea rolled in had a dog not discovered her.

Her shirt had ridden up a bit from Kate's initial exam.

'She looks anywhere between fourteen and twenty-one, I'd say,' Kate began. 'It's a bit more difficult to tell because she's been exposed to the elements I'd say she died from having the knife rammed into her eyeball. I'll be able to make a proper determination when I get her back to the mortuary.'

'Are those defence wounds?' Miller asked, keeping his hands in his pockets and nodding to the bruises on the girl's body.

'No. These are old scars, as if somebody had beaten her in the past.'

'Looks like somebody really hurt her.'

'Probably with a belt, or something like it,' Kate said.

'Poor girl,' Purcell said. He looked at the pathologist. 'Can you give us a rough estimate of TOD?'

'No more than twelve hours.'

'The forensics team have swept the beach. Did somebody take her fingerprints yet?'

Kate nodded. 'A little while ago.'

Miller took his hands out of his pockets for balance, making sure he didn't touch anything, merely pointing with a finger. 'Those earrings don't look cheap.'

Kim bent over and had a look. 'Impossible to tell whether or not the diamonds are fake.' She stood up. 'FYI, if that inspires my Christmas present, I don't do fake.'

'Duly noted.' Frank stood up. 'Is she ready to be transported? Gus Weaver and Sticks are waiting outside.' Sticks was one of the female mortuary attendants.

'Yes. You can let them in.'

Miller looked at the girl again. She had on tracksuit bottoms, and he wondered why she had been left down here. It was more than a mere robbery. No robber he'd ever known would have stopped to mutilate the victim.

Or it might indicate the earrings weren't diamonds at all. No, a robber wanted to steal, and there had been

8

fatalities during robberies of course, but this was more than a robbery gone wrong.

Gus Weaver, a man in his fifties, and Sticks, a Polish girl in her late twenties, came into the tent with a stretcher.

'You can load her up now, Gus,' Kate said.

'Get uniforms to help,' Purcell said, before he left the tent, and headed back to their cars on the promenade.

Miller started up his pool car and Kim jumped into the passenger seat for a moment.

'Frank, did you see those scars. Poor girl. Do you think this could have been parental abuse gone too far?'

'I'm thinking along that line. She has no ID on her though. We'll get her prints run through the system and see if she's a missing person, or anything else.'

'Who would do such a thing to a young woman like that?'

'There are a lot of people out there who would do that sort of thing.'

TWO

Ed 'Podge' Hamilton sat at his desk, looking out of the window down to Waverley station below. The new council building was down on Market Street, a far cry from the old eyesore that had sat on the corner of High Street and George IV Bridge. He worked in social services as a case manager, a job he didn't particularly enjoy but, the need to eat and keep a roof over his head, made him stick at it.

He watched as a train pulled into Waverley station below and wondered how many of the young people he dealt with had arrived via that method. Homeless youngsters, running away from something, heading to God knows where. A lot of kids ran away to London, but those already in the south had to have somewhere else to run to. Edinburgh was usually their destination.

Podge was supposed to be working but he had a more pressing issue on his mind; whether he should call Vicky or not. He was brought back to the here and now when his friend stopped by his door with the mail cart.

'Jesus. Why are you creeping about like that?' he asked. 'Twat.'

'It's called work, fuck face. Something you should try now and again.'

'Please. You wouldn't know how to spell *work*.'

The other man laughed. 'Why are you looking so glum, anyway?' Stumpy said. He was a small man who somebody had once said was no bigger than a tree stump, and although he could have taken offence, Mickey Wilson had thick skin. Everybody called him *Stumpy* and he wore it like a badge of honour.

'It's getting close to Christmas and I know the department is going on a shindig on Saturday night, but I haven't asked Vicky if she'll go with me.'

'Jesus. Is that all? You need *Uncle Stumpy's Guide to Pulling Women*.'

'Please. Your idea of how to pull a woman is to splash some *Old Spice* under your armpits in the toilets of a nightclub and hope she's too pished to say no.'

'That's it, let the anger out, and then when you've calmed down, you can listen to what Uncle Stumpy has to say.'

'You're three years older than me. Hardly uncle material, unless you're rich and going to pop your clogs any minute.'

Stumpy worked in the mailroom of the Edinburgh

Social Services department, while Podge was based in the offices. He walked into the room with a pile of mail for Podge.

'When I die, pal, there's going to be zero left in the bank. I'm not married, I have no kids, and I intend to die broke, but happy.'

'Well, on the pay this shower give us, you'll achieve that no problem.' Podge picked up a pencil and tapped his teeth. 'So, is this real mail you've got for me, or is this you just doing one of your *pretending to be working* runs?'

'How dare you. I hope you're not suggesting that I sit down in the mailroom giving that new lassie a bit of chat all day.'

'That's exactly what I'm suggesting.'

Stumpy took out a pile of mail from a slot in his cart. 'I keep that mailroom running single-handedly. That new lassie just needs to be taken under my wing and we'll get on like a house on fire. I might invite her to the Christmas party. Here, it says it's for the boss of the department, but you'll do.'

'Just give me the mail, for God's sake.'

Stumpy laughed and handed it over. 'So, your dilemma, I have a solution.'

'Go on then, inspire me.'

'Why don't you just *ask* Vicky?'

Podge looked like he hadn't thought of that. 'You might have a point there, Stumps.'

'And they call you *Brains* behind your back. Now I know why.'

'Do you think I should?'

'Of course. Why don't you come over with me to the Washington?' Washington House was a B-listed, red sandstone Victorian building, named after the Glaswegian architect who designed it in 1892, George Washington Browne. Formerly the sick kids hospital at the Grange, now a homeless charity had taken it over. Social services liaised with the charity and helped young homeless people find a home and a job.

'I don't know. I'm sort of busy. I don't know if I'll have time.'

'Nonsense. You're a manager. You can go over there anytime. She's over there all day. I spoke to her this morning. I have to go to the satellite mailroom and work there this afternoon, and you can come over. Then you can take her aside and ask her.'

'For a little man, you have some big ideas.'

'I told you, just listen to Uncle Stumpy.'

'If you were my uncle, I'd have you arrested.'

THREE

Detective Chief Inspector Paddy Gibb stood in front of the whiteboard in the incident room, Percy Purcell next to him.

'How's the fight with trying to give up smoking?' Miller said, walking up beside him.

'I swear to God I think I'll turn into a Polo mint if I even think about any more sweets.' He looked at Miller. 'It's been six days and I think I'm going to go on a rampage. I'm bad tempered, I can't sleep, and I have the shakes.'

'You get like that when you try and get your wallet out in the pub.'

'That's true, but the end result is, somebody buys me a drink.' Gibb put his hand in his pocket and felt the unopened packet of cigarettes there. It had been months since he'd smoked a full pack in a day, cutting back slowly.

'How's things with you and your girlfriend?' Purcell said.

'Girlfriend. Christ, I'm in my fifties and I have a girlfriend. It makes me feel like I'm sixteen again. But luckily she's very understanding. When they asked me to stay on until the spring and then retire, I was in two minds. I know they're short with you doing the work of Dennis Friendly and David Elliot, Bruce will be off until God knows when, and Hazel's off on early maternity leave. But we can't go away until next spring anyway, so she's happy enough.'

'Don't let the stress get to you, Paddy. You want to enjoy your retirement.'

'I know, sir. One bastard went out to mow his lawn, came back into the house and died in his armchair.' He took his hand out of his pocket, letting go of the cigarettes. Drank some of the coffee he was holding. 'We're not getting very far with this young girl. No ID, nothing on her prints.'

'We're widening the search now, Paddy. I have our boys checking out local CCTV, see if we can see somebody dumping her there.'

'Less than two weeks until Christmas and somebody's going to get a Christmas to remember for all the wrong reasons,' Purcell said.

'I think she was a runaway. She came from somewhere. See all those scars on her?' Miller pointed to the photos on the board. 'If she's a youngster, then she might have come from an abusive home.'

'That's one way to look at it.'

'From where I'm standing, Paddy, that's the only way to look at it.'

One of the younger detectives, Jimmy Gilmour, shouted from across the room. 'It's for you, sir.' He indicated to Miller, holding the phone up.

Miller walked across and took it. 'Hello?'

'This is Fiona up at the lab.'

'Oh, hi, Fiona.'

'I had a look at the earrings the girl was wearing when you found her on the beach. They're real diamonds.'

'Can you fax over a photo of them?'

'Sure, I'll do it right away. Or I can email the photo.'

'It's for Paddy Gibb.'

'Fax it is then.'

'I'm assuming they're expensive?'

'Let me put it to you this way, I would be impressed if a man gave me a pair.'

'And it takes a lot to impress you, Fiona.'

'I don't know if I've just been insulted or not.'

'I wouldn't insult you. I'm just inferring that you have good taste.'

'You're digging yourself a deeper hole here, Frank.'

'And with that, I'll thank you for calling. Oh, are you going to the night out on Saturday?'

'Try and stop me.'

'See you there.'

'Just remember, I was talking with Kim earlier, so I don't want any shenanigans with the mistletoe like last year.'

'As if.'

Frank hung up and walked back over to the whiteboard. 'The earrings the girl was wearing are real diamonds.'

'So she has a boyfriend who has a big wallet,' Purcell said.

'Maybe not a big wallet, but a big shotgun.'

'What?' Gibb said.

'See this.' Miller went over to another part of the room where there was a whiteboard on one wall. On it were photos of items of jewellery. 'I don't know why this didn't occur to me before.' He tapped one of the photos. 'In the robbery at *Humphries the Jewellers* a couple of weeks ago, the guy took a load of high-end watches, but he also stopped to take a pair of earrings. These look like the earrings that were on the girl.'

'Jesus. I wasn't leaning towards the girl's murder being a robbery, and this rather confirms my point. Any robber worth his salt would take the jewellery. He would have had a quick squint to see if she had anything of any value in her ears.'

'I'm thinking we have a vicious killer on our hands, Paddy. He wasn't interested in the earrings.'

'Somebody gave her those. It looks like she knew him.' He pointed to a still from the store where a robber had walked in two weeks ago and relieved them of numerous watches. Miller remembered watching the footage as the man had smashed a cabinet with earrings in it, reached in and pulled out a pair.

Jimmy Gilmour walked over and handed Gibb the fax copy of the photo of the earrings Fiona had sent over. 'This is for you, sir.'

'Thanks, Jimmy.' Gilmour walked away. 'Andy?'

DS Andy Watt turned round to look at his boss. He was an older detective, in his early fifties, whose rise up the career ladder had been impeded by his sharp tongue. 'Yes?' No *sir* was added.

'You're working the jewellery store detail, aren't you?'

'I am.'

'How far along are you with it?'

'We're cross-referencing it with robberies in other parts of Scotland. There was a similar one in Aberdeen, but we don't think it's connected.'

'Okay. Thanks.'

'I'll make some phone calls, get them to work harder on that angle, just in case,' Purcell said.

'Maybe this girl is part of a gang,' Gibb said.

'If she was part of a gang, why would they murder her?'

'I've never been a believer in the old cliché about there being honour among thieves. Maybe she was surplus to requirements.'

'That was a brutal way to get rid of her.' Miller

walked over to the vending machine and popped in a few coins for a coffee. 'Anybody want one?'

Gibb shook his head.

'I'll have one,' Watt said, from the other side of the room, grinning like an idiot.

'When was the last time you put your hand in your pocket, Andy?' Purcell said.

'When you could get change out of a ten bob note,' Gibb said.

'You would know,' Watt said, in a low voice.

In her role with the procurator fiscal's office, Dr Kim Smith spent more time in the High Street station than up in the Crown Office department in the Sheriff Court building. She had a small office in the investigation suite, off the incident room.

She was working at her desk when Miller knocked and she told him to come in.

'How's Hazel doing?' he asked. DS Hazel Carter was part of Miller's team, currently on maternity leave. Her boyfriend, DS Bruce Hagan, was on extended medical leave after being abducted by a serial killer and tortured a few months earlier, and now Hazel was only a couple of months away from giving birth.

'She's stressing out, Frank. She hurts when she walks. She has horrendous back pain, her ankles swell, and she's dog tired. She also has piles.'

'Jesus, Kim. I'll never look at Hazel the same way again.'

She laughed. 'She's struggling to finish her Christmas shopping for Bruce and Jane.'

'Jane will be happy with some toys, I'm sure.'

'Struggling physically, Frank, not for ideas. I said I would drive her down to Kinnaird Park on Saturday morning. I'll use your Audi if you don't mind?'

'First of all, it's ours, and secondly, your dad got it for Jack. You know you can take it whenever you want.'

Kim looked at him with a sly smile. 'We're still talking about the car, right?'

'Honey, at this moment in time, I couldn't love you any more. However, as much as your dirty talk pleases me, I have to go and talk to a man about a robbery.'

'Okay. But one thing before you go.'

'Shoot.'

'I didn't know you last Christmas, but I heard about your carry-on with Fiona from the lab and the piece of mistletoe.'

'It's all lies.'

'No, it's not. Look at you. Standing there trying to wriggle out of this. Fiona herself told me when the girls had a night out a few weeks ago.'

Miller felt his face going red. 'It was just a bit of harmless fun.'

Kim laughed. 'I know it was, silly. I'm just pulling your leg.'

'Rest assured the only mistletoe will be hanging above your head this year.'

'Under the thumb already, boss?' Andy Watt said, coming up behind Miller.

'Me? Behave yourself. I'm my own man, Andy.' He winked at Kim.

'You should have asked her permission to say that.'

Miller shook his head and closed Kim's door. 'Right, Andy, you're with me.'

Watt grabbed his jacket off the back of his chair and followed Miller out of the office.

FOUR

'Are you sure about this, Stumpy?' Podge asked, as they walked along the corridor of Washington House, Stumpy carrying a mailbag; the building housing numerous offices, as well as the dorms.

'Of course, I'm sure,' he said, handing Podge the mailbag as he stopped by a vending machine outside the canteen doors, popping money in for a bar of chocolate. 'You want one?'

'No. I used to be twice this size, hence the nickname, *Podge.* I don't intend going back to that. Unlike you, who could do with losing a few.'

'This is a solid wall of muscle,' he said, patting his stomach. 'Go on, take your best shot.'

'Oh, yeah, that would look good, me punching a man who's only five foot one.'

Stumpy laughed and made his selection. 'No, mate,

listen to Uncle Stumps, Vicky wants you to ask her out.'

'She might think I'm a pervert who's been stalking her.'

'Will you give over? Look, I've seen the way she looks at you. Her eyes couldn't shine any brighter.'

'Maybe I'll be in with a chance then.'

'Steady, you're only going to ask her to the dance, not whip it out in front of her.'

Stumpy picked out his bar of chocolate and unwrapped it, taking the mailbag back.

'What if I ask her and get all tongue tied?'

'For God's sake, just be yourself. Oh, wait; you're an obnoxious twat. Don't be yourself; pretend to be nice.'

'Piss off.'

'That's it, get a bit of practise in before we get up there.'

They started walking towards the lift. 'I wish I hadn't listened to you. Uncle fucking Stumpy. You would have been the eighth dwarf if they'd remade the movie. This was a wasted trip.'

They stepped in and took it up to admin on the fourth floor. 'Just as well I'm not thin skinned. I'm sure you've just broken all sorts of disability laws there. Dwarfs are called *little people* now. Ignoramus.'

'I'm just nervous, Stumps. I don't know why. We go out at the weekend and always manage to pull a couple of women.'

Stumpy stopped and looked at his friend. 'First of all, they're wasted by the time we ask them to dance. Second, I do the talking while you sit there slavering, and by the time they play Eric Clapton's *Wonderful Tonight*, you're about ready to be poured into a taxi.'

'Pish. I'm always up on the dance floor giving it what for.'

They started walking to the offices again. 'Vicky's probably been waiting all day for you to ask her to the night out,' Stumpy said, as they rounded the corner.

'We'll find out shortly, won't we?'

FIVE

Brian Hall strode along the top level of Washington House, clutching a folder under his arm. Somebody had once told him, *If you're walking about looking busy, nobody will ever question you.*

Now he was heading for his favourite bolthole. Maybe get his feet up for a snooze before heading off for a pint at lunchtime.

Then he saw her, coming towards him. Vicky was her name. He'd had his eye on her for a while now, watching her, waiting for the right moment to talk to her. She was holding a pile of folders. Timing was everything.

As she made to pass him, he bumped her, knocking the files from her arms.

'Oh my goodness, I'm so sorry,' he said, feigning concern. 'Look how clumsy I am.'

'It's no problem,' she said.

'Let me get them for you.' He picked them up, shuffling the errant papers back inside the folders. 'Again, I'm sorry. My name's Brian, by the way.' He held out a hand for her to shake, smiling at her.

'I'm Vicky.' She smiled back at him.

I know. 'I've seen you around here before, but I've never had the chance to introduce myself. What a first impression though.'

She gave a small laugh. 'I've seen worse.'

'I'm new here. Jack of all trades. Do this, do that. You name it; I can turn my hand to it.'

'You're a handy man, then. If you'll pardon the pun.'

'If you ever need anything done at home, I'm your man. Cheaper than a rip-off tradesman.' The truth was, he barely knew which end of a hammer to use, but the object of the exercise was to get close to her and what better place than her own home?

He beamed his best smile at her, knowing that was one of his best features. He'd spent good money to have his teeth fixed and it had paid him back on more than one occasion.

'Well, I have to run. It was nice meeting you, Brian.'

'Nice meeting you too. Maybe we could have a coffee if I bump into you in the canteen.'

'Maybe.' She smiled and walked away.

She's interested in you if she looks back. She turned the corner without looking back. *Fuck.* Never mind. She *was* interested in him. She just didn't know it yet.

SIX

There were two times of the year when Edinburgh was off its head with visitors; in August with the International Festival, and Christmas. It took Miller and Watt twenty minutes to get from their office in the station, down to *Humphries the Jewellers* in George Street. They managed to get a space on double yellow lines and Miller put the *Police Business* card in the windscreen.

'How you doing after last week?' Watt said, referring to an incident Miller had been involved in the week before. He'd been called to an office block after a gunman had taken hostages and demanded to talk with Miller. He'd also been a suicide bomber.

'I'm fine. If it had turned out differently, I might not have been.'

'This is the new flagship store,' Watt said, as they

went in through the door. There was a security guard on duty. A young woman came forward and smiled.

'Can I help you find anything today?'

Miller and Watt showed their warrant cards. 'We'd like to speak to the manager.'

'I'll go and get him.' She turned and walked away.

The store was on three levels, open from the top level down to the lower ground floor. Miller looked over the banister at the cases below, no doubt filled with jewellery worth more than he earned in a year. Watt was leaning backwards, craning his head to look up.

Miller strolled over to a glass cabinet filled with expensive watches, sorted by make.

'Those earrings that lassie had on, they were expensive,' Watt said, joining him.

'They have nice pieces in here.'

'No doubt young Kim will be dragging you here on your day off sometime soon. Better get the overtime in.'

'We're not in a rush, Andy.'

'You should be.'

'Why's that?'

'Look what happened to Hagan. He's messed up now. God knows when he'll be fit for active duty again.' Watt looked at his boss. 'You never know what's round the corner. Look at me; I'm fifty-three next year, divorced and living in a rented flat. So I was thinking one day, is this how it's going to be for the rest of my life? Wasting away until all I have to look forward to in retirement is coming home and opening a can of dog food?'

'Jesus, Andy, you'll retire with a fair pension. You'll be able to live off Heinz beans at least.'

'I'm not talking about not having money to buy food; I'm talking about being arsed cooking. Sit down with a can of Pedigree Chum and get my feet up to watch *Coronation Street*. That's not the life for me, Frank.'

'I can see why a retirement home wouldn't use that as a selling point, right enough.'

'I want to go through life with somebody. So when I eventually become a grandpa, the wee ones won't be coming round to the smelly old bastard on Christmas Day, dying to get away after they've been given their selection boxes.'

'Or their bag of dog treats.'

'Exactly. So that's why I went on one of those dating sites. *Love Interest dot com*. Let me tell you, it was a mate of mine who pointed me in that direction. He tried it, and got himself a nice woman. I thought it would all be bunny boilers, but there's a lot of cracking divorcees on there.'

'Have you met anybody?'

'I have. Her name's Jean, she's divorced and has a married son. And a little granddaughter as well.' He looked wistfully towards the engagement ring section. 'I wish my two lassies would hurry up and give me a wee ankle biter.'

'How many times you been out with her? And why haven't I found out about this before?'

'I was hedging my bets. If she turned out to be a complete howler, then nobody would find out.'

'I hope you treat her well when you're out with her. *Howler*. Good God.'

'She's not a howler, well, not in the looks department, anyway. And I'm going to see her on Saturday night after the work's Christmas party.'

'Why didn't you just invite her along?'

'And have you bunch of reprobates lusting after her? No, thank you.'

'Andy, I'm hardly going to be lusting after your girl-friend, especially since my own will be there.'

'Not you. Gibb. His wife kicked him into touch a long time ago, and believe me, he's been out with plenty of howlers. If he saw Jean, he'd be splashing on the Old Spice and sucking a mint, hoping he could persuade her to dump me and hook up with him.'

'I don't think Paddy's a relationship wrecker.'

'I don't know, boss. Have you seen the way he takes out his packet of cigarettes and looks at them? You would think he was looking at a photo of his kids. He's not right upstairs.' Watt said, tapping the side of his head.

'He's trying to give up smoking and finding it difficult.'

They moved over to a case displaying watches.

'They're nice, but how can anybody justify the expense of that?' Watt said.

'Some people collect watches. They're an investment.'

'Look at that. Omega Seamaster GMT. Seven grand.'

'It's a nice watch, Andy.'

They heard somebody approaching from behind. 'Can I help you, officers?'

'DI Miller. DS Watt. And you are?'

'Cecil Cavendish. I'm the manager.'

'Can we talk somewhere privately?'

Cavendish took them through to the back of the store, into his office. They sat down. He only looked a few years older than Miller, but his haircut probably cost more than Miller earned in a month.

'We're following up on the robbery,' Miller said, noting that the office had the same ambience as the store itself.

'Fire away.'

'We were looking at stills from the CCTV, and we wanted to ask you if there was anything else you remembered about the robber?'

'Such as?' Cavendish said, spreading his hands on the desk in front of him, as if he was expecting hand-cuffs to be slapped on them.

'You said in your statement that you chased the robber outside. Did you see anybody else with him?'

Cavendish sat back. 'No. He ran across Castle Street and out of sight.'

Watt looked at him. 'Do you think it could have been a woman?'

'A woman? No, it didn't sound like a woman. It was the rough voice of a man.' He looked at Miller. 'What makes you think it was a woman?'

'We found a woman, deceased, wearing similar earrings to the ones that were stolen from here. We think they're the actual ones.' Miller pulled out the photo of the earrings and passed it over.

'A dead woman was wearing them?' He looked at the photo and nodded. 'Yes, these are the ones.'

'How can you be so sure?'

'They were made exclusively for us. I'm ninety per cent sure, but I'd have to look at them in person. They would have our stamp on them.' He made a face. 'Try and sell them now after a dead woman had them. How did she get them, anyway?'

'That's something we're working on. Can you tell us more about them?'

'They were designed for us by an Edinburgh designer, Gina Rosales. She's one of the best up-and-coming jewellery designers in the UK. They're eighteen carat white gold, the stones being point eight carats. They were worth three and a half thousand pounds.'

'Could you give us Ms Rosales' contact details?'

'Yes, I can.' He opened a desk drawer and rummaged about, bringing out a small notebook. He flicked through until he found the page he wanted then noted down the address on a pad, ripped off the sheet, and passed it over to Miller. 'As you can see, she lives locally.'

Miller noted it was a New Town address.

He and Watt stood. 'Thank you for your help, Mr Cavendish.'

Outside, Miller took out his mobile phone as they got in the car. He called Gina Rosales' number.

'Hello, this is Detective Inspector Frank Miller. I'm looking for Gina Rosales.'

'You found her.' Despite the Italian name, the voice was very much Scottish.

'I was wondering when it would be a good time to talk to you.'

'What about?'

'Your designs.'

'Okay. I work from home if you want to come round now.'

'Mr Cavendish from *Humphries* gave me your address. We're at George Street right now. We won't be long.'

'I'll have the kettle on.'

Miller looked at his phone as she cut the connection.

'Where we off to, boss?' Watt said.

'Just down the road.'

Watt pulled away, honking the horn at a man

dressed in a Santa outfit who had stepped out in front of him.

Santa started walking towards the driver's side.

Watt rolled the window down. Held up the police sign. 'Go on then, Santa, and I'll give you a Christmas you'll never forget.'

Santa stopped and then thought better of it. Waited until he was over the other side of the road before giving Watt the finger.

'Not much chance of picking him out of a line-up, is there?' Miller said, as Watt drove away.

SEVEN

Vicky walked away from Brian Hall and didn't look over her shoulder as she rounded the corner. She knew he'd still be standing there. Watching her.

She supposed he was nice enough, but inviting him round to wallpaper the fireplace wall? No chance.

She let out a small yell as she almost bumped into Podge and Stumpy. 'Oh, boys. I didn't see you there.'

'Is everything okay?' Podge asked.

'Oh, yes, I was just daydreaming. Let's go in here.' She led them into the admin offices and closed the door behind her.

There were several empty office cubicles, and she just needed a room with a chair and PC to get her paperwork processed.

'How's things, Vicky?' Stumpy said, putting his mailbag down on the floor. 'Bloody freezing out there, eh?'

Vicky laughed. 'Well, it is December, Stumpy.'

'You may have a point there, Miss Vicky. I'll get the kettle on.'

'There isn't one anymore.'

'What? No kettle,' Podge said. 'Aren't you allowed to make a cuppa now?'

'It's Health and Safety. The kettle has to be processed by an electrician, to make sure it's safe. Otherwise it might get on fire and burn the building down.'

'It's PC gone mad, I tell you.'

'There's a machine down in the canteen. I'm due a break, so why don't I take you boys down and buy you a coffee?'

'Oh, here, we don't want you letting the moths out of your purse,' Stumpy said.

'Cheeky wee monkey,' Vicky said, laughing.

Podge looked at her and thought about being alone with her. She was in her late thirties, but looked ten years younger.

They rode the lift down to the ground floor and went along to the canteen, then sat at a table with their coffees.

'Podge here wanted to ask you something,' Stumpy said.

'Oh, is that right, Podge? Well, ask away. I'm all ears.'

Podge could feel his face starting to go red. 'Well,

actually, I wanted to say... well, I just wanted to know if you were going to the dance with anybody.'

She smiled at him. 'No, I'm not.' She reached a hand over to Stumpy's and squeezed. 'And you boys were wanting to escort me there. Am I right?'

Aw, fuck off, Podge thought. I should have just come out and asked her, but now look what I've done. 'That's right, me and Stumpy were wondering if we could take you to the night out. Just so you don't feel alone.'

'Oh, I'd love that. Thank you so much. I have to admit, I wasn't going to go, but now I've got my best pals going with me, I will.'

Stumpy looked at Podge like *How did you fuck that up?* Podge just shrugged at his friend.

The smile fell from Vicky's face as she looked over Podge's shoulder. Stumpy turned to see what she was looking at.

A man was standing looking at them. He smiled and waved at Vicky. She smiled, more of a grimace, and waved back.

'Who's that?' Stumpy asked. Podge tried nonchalantly to look round. He saw the man sitting down with a cup of coffee. Facing Vicky.

'It's just a man who works here,' she said.

'His name's Brian,' Podge said. 'He started talking to me one day when I was working on one of the computers, and now every time I come in, he treats me as if I'm his best friend. He seems harmless enough.'

Podge looked up. 'Oh shite, here he comes now. Pardon the language.'

'Hi, Ed,' Hall said. 'How are you?'

'I'm fine, Brian. What are you up to?'

'Just doing things.' He looked at Vicky and smiled. 'Hello, again.'

'Hello.' Vicky couldn't make eye contact with him.

'I'm having a Christmas party, Ed. I'd like you to come,' Hall said, beaming a smile.

'I'll think about it and get back to you, Brian.'

'Great. You can both come.' He nodded at Vicky then looked at Stumpy. 'Are you one of Santa's elves?'

'No I'm fu—' Stumpy started to say, but Podge held up a hand.

'No, he works with us,' he said, trying not to laugh.

'Okay. Let me know about the party. Bye.' He turned and wandered away.

'Cheeky bastard,' Stumpy said.

Podge was grinning. 'He's probably one of those special needs workers. He doesn't know what he's saying.'

'I'll bet he fucking does. He can shove his party up his arse.'

Podge laughed as they finished their coffee. 'I don't believe you were invited.'

EIGHT

Watt parked in front of the mews house in Dublin Street Lane. They shivered in the cold as wind whipped along the road, remnants from the last snowfall stubbornly clinging to the edges of doorways and the bottom of downspouts. It was an old property that had been given the benefit of a refit and looked very upscale. As did the woman who answered the door.

'Gina Rosales?' Miller asked, as they showed their warrant cards.

'Indeed I am. Please come in.' She stood back until the detectives had entered. They were in a hallway with stairs ahead of them. 'Please go on up. The living room is up there.'

Upstairs, the living room was open plan, with a kitchen against the back wall and an office area facing them.

'Coffee, gentlemen?'

'That would be nice, thanks,' Miller said. 'Black.'

'For me, too,' Watt said.

Miller saw several drawings stuck on a wallboard next to the desk, sketches of pieces of jewellery; rings and earrings taking centre stage.

Gina poured them their coffees and they stood at the kitchen island separating the kitchen area from the living room.

'This is a nice place you have here,' Watt said.

'Thank you. It was falling apart before I bought it, and I had a company come in and make it like brand new.' She smiled at Watt.

Gina was in her thirties, he guessed, with short, blonde hair, expensively styled. Although she was wearing jeans and a shirt, he could tell they were expensive.

'So what have I done that warrants a visit from the local police?' she said, smiling.

'We're interested in a design you did for *Humphries*.'

'Oh, really? Which one?'

Miller showed her the photo of the earrings. 'This one.'

She looked at it and smiled. 'Ah, the Clara Collection. It's been one of their best sellers.'

'Despite the price,' Watt said, sipping his coffee.

'*Humphries* isn't one of your shopping centre jewellers, so they are indeed pricey, But not to the people who can afford them.' Her smile stayed in place the whole time she was talking. 'You'd be surprised at what people are willing to pay for exquisite jewellery.'

'So these earrings are part of a collection?' Miller said, putting the photo away.

'Yes. Earrings, a necklace, and bracelet.' She drank more of her coffee. 'Can I ask why you're interested in those earrings?'

'They were found on a murder victim.'

Gina's smiled dropped. 'Oh, no! Were they the ones stolen from the store last week?'

'Yes, they were. What makes you ask that?'

'Because they're a new line and Cecil told me there had been interest in the collection, and although they can be bought as a three-piece set, none have been sold yet. Only the necklaces have sold, and none of the earrings.'

'Do you sell them anywhere else?' Watt asked.

'Oh, I only do the design, but they're exclusive.'

'How long have you been designing for *Humphries*?'

'A little over six years.'

'Do you know Cecil Cavendish well?' Watt said.

'Yes, I do. We work well together.'

'The thing we were wondering is, why would the robber just take those earrings? He stole a whole load of high-end watches, and there were cabinets full of necklaces and earrings, yet he smashed one cabinet and just took that pair.'

'It does seem strange.'

'It was as if they were targeted,' Watt said, looking for a reaction and getting none.

'Obviously, whoever robbed the store has good taste.'

Miller put his cup down. 'Thanks for the coffee, Ms Rosales. If you can think of anything that might be helpful, we'd appreciate a call.' He handed over a business card.

'I'll be sure to call if I think of anything.'

Watt put his cup down as well, and thanked her.

Outside, snowflakes were gently falling as the temperature had dropped.

'What do you think of her?' Miller asked, as they got back in the car, Watt behind the wheel again.

'Well, I wouldn't climb over her to get to you, if that's what you mean.'

'It's not. And you wish.'

'She's very nice. I don't think she robbed the place, though.'

'Me neither. It still doesn't explain why the thief targeted those earrings.'

'Maybe he didn't.'

'What do you mean, Andy?'

'What if he was just in there for the watches and decided to nick a pair on the way out, maybe for a girlfriend?'

'You might have a point.'

But his gut was telling him something else.

NINE

'I wonder how my dad's getting on?' He and Kim were snuggled up on the sofa watching TV, Kim feeling more content than she ever had. Emma was in the corner of the living room, playing with her dolls and the dolls' house Miller had bought her. Charlie, the cat, was sleeping nearby.

'What's not to love about Christmas in New York? Samantha's showing him around and he told me in his last email they had been on a carriage ride in Central Park. A wee Irish bloke was driving it. I'm glad he and Sam made it through that bad patch last summer. They're right for each other.'

'I know they are. His friends are envious that he's going out with a famous crime writer. *The* Samantha Willis? they always say when I tell people.'

'And he's the one paying for *her* to go back home. Nobody can say he's only after her money.'

'He's got a few notes socked away, especially after he finally sold his house.'

'Do you think he and Sam will buy a place together?'

'I don't know. They're having a good time just now. Time will tell for them.'

'I wonder if they'll get married?'

'Maybe they will, but he hasn't even moved in with her. Living along the hallway from us just makes it easy for him to see her. Why? Is it starting to bother you that he's still here with us?'

She pulled away from him. 'No, of course not. He was living with you long before I came on the scene.' She snuggled back down. '*EastEnders*, honey, if you don't mind.'

Miller flipped through the channels until he came to BBC.

'I know this isn't exciting for you, being a Friday night and stuck in with me,' she said.

'We've been through this, how many times now? I turned thirty-three months ago, and I'm at home with my family. I don't need to go out boozing with my pals every weekend anymore.'

'I know, honey. Sometimes it's my old insecurities coming back. I was alone with Emma for a few years after I got divorced, while her father swanned about with any girl who would go with him. I went out on dates, of course, but as soon as they found out I had a child, they couldn't get away fast enough.'

'Well, I'm in this for the long haul.' He watched the TV for a second. 'I got an email from Percy Purcell. He and Suzie are engaged. He asked her on her birthday, back in October. In the spring, they'll get hitched.'

'Get *hitched*? How romantic, Miller.'

He had been going to say, *shackled* but had thought better of it at the last minute. As the soap played out, he started thinking about the rings in *Humphries* and whether his salary would stretch to one in there.

Then his thoughts jumped to the dead girl they'd found on the beach. The news on TV had shown a sketch of the girl his department had done, but they'd kept the fact about her wearing expensive earrings to themselves, just in case somebody made a confession, then if he added the bit about the jewellery, they would know he was genuine.

'You still seeing Hazel on Saturday for your shopping trip?' he asked her.

'Yes. My mum's taking Emma over to Jenners to the toy department. To see the sort of stuff that Santa makes.'

He wondered if a mother out there somewhere was missing her daughter. Then he pictured the scars on the poor girl's body. Probably not.

TEN

I stand looking out my living room window and take a sip of the cognac in my hand. St Stephen's Church stands opposite, the clock in its clock tower telling me it's almost time to go out. I'm wired after exercising in the little gym I've made in the spare room. Just a treadmill and a weights bench but it makes me feel like I'm keeping fit.

I'm lucky; this is one of the penthouse apartments, much bigger than the others on the lower level, so there's room for my equipment.

Keeping healthy is important to me. I have to maintain a certain level of fitness for my lifestyle.

I see her approaching my back, her reflection clear in the window. She wraps her arms around my waist.

'I want you right now,' she says, her perfume heady, her breath light against the back of my neck.

I smile and turn to face her, putting my glass down

on the narrow table next to the window. I grab her face with both hands and kiss her hard, feeling her back arch and her breathing increase.

She walks backwards until the edge of the settee catches the back of her legs and she falls, but I don't let her go. I strip her, my body eager to be with hers and we make love right there on the settee. Afterwards, the woman dresses quickly and I head for the shower.

'The money's on the table,' I tell her. 'Same as last time.'

'Thanks, sweetheart. Call me when you need me again.'

She leaves the flat, closing the door softly behind her. After my shower, I dress for going out.

I walk across to the dressing table and open the top drawer. Select one of my new watches.

It's a Jaeger-LeCoultre Master Ultra Thin 1907. The rose gold case with the brown alligator strap. It's refined elegance. And cost me a fortune, but I had to have it.

I slip it on and put on my heavy overcoat. I leave the Porsche downstairs in the underground garage, not wanting to draw attention to myself by being drunk behind the wheel. That's the last thing I want. Although it'll be gone soon. I don't care though. Soon, all my worries will be behind me.

I shiver inside the overcoat and am glad I've put on the woollen hat. Edinburgh's hardly the Arctic Circle, but it gets cold enough.

The walk to my destination will take me fifteen minutes as it's all uphill. In the snow. Though the snow is pretty much gone from the pavements, just remnants of it lying about in the gutters.

I ease my pace as I get near the house I'm aiming for, not wanting to be out of breath when I get there. I want to have energy before we go out. Maybe if I play my cards right, I can make love to her before we hit the town. The whore has just whetted my appetite, and now I'm going to see the fucking whore I don't have to pay for.

I force the smile on my face before I ring the doorbell. I hear her faffing about with the lock on her front door. Hurry up, you stupid cow, it's freezing out here. I'm gritting my teeth.

Then the door is open. And I smile.

'Come on in,' Gina Rosales says, stepping to one side.

ELEVEN

The next morning, it was cold enough for more snow, but the sky was clear as Miller walked up High Street to the station, pulling the collar up on his overcoat. Kim was taking Emma to school before going to her own office.

It was warm inside and Miller decided to grab a coffee from the machine before he did anything else.

'You've got a visitor,' the desk sergeant said, nodding to a man sitting on the bench in the reception area.

'Are you Inspector Miller?' the man said, and Miller took his hands out of his pockets.

'I am. And you are?'

'Ed Hamilton.'

'And what can I do for you, Mr Hamilton?'

'It's about that young girl who was murdered.'

Miller gave the desk sergeant a look. No words

were needed. Next thing, a uniform came out from behind the public counter, in case Hamilton started trouble and needed restraining.

'You have information for us?' *Or are you here just to confess?*

'I do.'

'Okay. This way.'

Miller led the way upstairs, Hamilton and the uniform following behind. Miller showed Hamilton into an interview room and told him to wait. He returned with Andy Watt, and the uniform remained inside the room by the door.

'So what is this information you have for us, Mr Hamilton?'

'Everybody calls me Podge. It's a nickname. You can call me that if you like.'

'Mr Hamilton will be fine,' Watt said.

'Right. So I saw on the news about the murder of that young girl.'

'Do you know her?'

'No. I saw her. At least I think it was her.'

Miller and Watt exchanged a look. 'Go on.'

'I saw her a couple of weeks ago, getting into a van. I remember because she just swung the door open and it banged into me. Then she cursed me out, telling me to watch what I was doing. Cheeky cow.' He looked at Miller. 'God rest her soul.'

'What makes you so sure it was her?' Watt said.

'As I said, I'm not a hundred per cent sure. But she

spoke with a Brummie accent. You know, from Birmingham?'

'I know what a Brummie is,' Miller said. 'Did you get a look at the registration plate?'

'No, but I got a good look at the driver. And I know his name.'

Miller sat up straighter in his chair. 'Give me the details.' He had his pen poised over the writing pad in front of him.

'His name's Brian Hall and he works at Washington House, the homeless shelter.'

Miller scribbled down the details.

'How do you know this man?' Watt asked.

'I work for social services as a case manager down in Market Street. I have to go over to other hospitals and homeless shelters, along with other members of staff. So I cadged a lift with one of the mailroom boys as he was going over too. A member of my staff was already there, to sort out clerical stuff, and we all had a coffee.'

Miller and Watt were waiting patiently for him to get to the point.

'Anyway, Brian Hall, who's new there, he's always talking to me when I'm there. I've seen him around plenty of times and he'll let on and talk as if I'm his new best friend. But Vicky said this bloke asked her out. She said there was something about him that she couldn't put her finger on.'

'And you think this man murdered the girl we found?'

'When I was in town, that girl opened the van door and it hit me. She told me to be careful, like it was my fault. I looked at the driver and I thought I'd seen him somewhere, and when I saw the identikit drawing of the girl, I knew I'd seen her with someone. It was him. Hall.'

'Where did you see them in this van?' Watt asked.

'In Young Street, off North Castle Street. I was meeting a pal of mine for lunch.'

'Did he say anything to you?'

'Not then, no, but I've seen him since then, and he talks to me.'

They questioned Podge further but there was evidently nothing more to add to the story, so they took his details and checked his ID before sending him on his way.

'What do you make of that?' Watt said, as they were standing at the coffee machine.

'I think we should track down this Brian Hall and have a little talk with him.'

TWELVE

Brian Hall walked along the corridor of the administration level of Washington House and smiled to himself. That was the beauty of people thinking you were a lowlife nobody; they didn't see you. It was almost as if he was a ghost, haunting the corridors of an asylum.

Although they weren't called asylums nowadays. It was called the *Psychiatric Hospital.* The State Hospital was out in the countryside, a place his mother always threatened him with.

A place his grandmother had called *The Farm.*

Do you want to go to The Farm? she would say, if he started acting up. He would just shake his head and tell her how sorry he was, picturing in his mind an axe splitting her skull in two. This was before he ended up in the young offenders' institution.

Now he walked along here, unseen, because the people who were so far up themselves didn't see him.

He wondered what they would think if they knew he'd been put away in the young persons' prison when he was a teenager. That would be his chance of making the lawn tennis team kicked into touch.

He couldn't care less that they looked past him, looked right *through* him, didn't acknowledge him in any way. Most of them. The only one who had given him the time of day was Vicky. Sweet little Vicky, with the drop-dead smile and the sunshine eyes.

He could feel his breathing start to get faster just thinking about her.

And let's not forget Ed Hamilton. Well, that was because he, Brian, had practically forced friendship on Hamilton.

He walked through a door marked *Personnel Only* and found the little room where the staff took breaks. He took out his newspaper and started to read. This was where he escaped to when he was trying to dodge doing any work. Being a maintenance engineer—a *gofer,* in other parlance—meant being at their beck and call; push this, pull that, sweep this. He did it though, without any complaints. He didn't want to lose his temper and have them send him somewhere like *that* place again.

His mother had wept as the police people took him away, the last time he had ever seen her. *Not fit to be in society,* he'd heard one social worker say about him, when he thought Hall wasn't listening. *He'll need to go to base camp.*

Base camp. What the hell was that? he'd thought. Base camp was a moniker that those smarmy, overpaid, brain-dead weasels called Wardrop House. *What kind of a fucking name was that anyway?*

He soon found out what Wardrop House was; something that had been teleported back from the nineteenth century. Correctly termed a young offenders Secure Accommodation Unit. Like a prison for underage kids. Filled with big bruising warders, with hands like shovels. They looked like extras in a horror movie. And every one of them with a fucking attitude.

They'd bent him into shape, with promises of a lobotomy and a stiff kicking if he talked about the place. His testicles still tingled even now, when he thought about the steel toecaps that had found their way there.

But they hadn't broken him.

He'd been a good actor though. *That* was the way to beat the bastards. No actor on Broadway had ever given a better performance than Brian Hall had. They thought he was just another scumbag passing through on his way to a life of prison.

Wardrop House had been his home until he reached adulthood and it had taught him nothing, if not how to play coy. Look and act as if you're daft. It never once occurred to Hall that he was indeed *actually* daft. Not *rocking back and forward talking to Jesus* kind of daft, but not having the mental capacity to differentiate between right and wrong. Not knowing where the line was, between taking the hint to go away, and smacking somebody in the throat with a broken bottle.

Hall walked a fine line. It was knowing not to cross it that kept him from being put away again.

It didn't stop him from looking though, did it?

THIRTEEN

Heather Dougal was the manager of Washington House, a woman with a large chest and hair pulled back in a bun. She smiled. 'What can I do for you?'

They were sitting in her office on the fourth floor.

'We need to speak to a man who works here. I don't know any details about him, like what times he works, or where he lives. I was wondering if you could help us,' Miller said, willing to bet the woman wasn't married.

'Give me his name and I'll find out.'

'Brian Hall.'

Heather looked at him before answering. 'He's here. Brian's working this morning. I saw him earlier.'

'Can you tell me what he does here?'

'Brian is a maintenance engineer. It means he does odd jobs around here and helps out down at our ware-house. Helping to load the van and things like that.'

'He keeps busy, then?'

'He does. He's a great asset.'

'I'd like to speak to him.'

She looked at the clock on the wall. 'He'll be around somewhere. We don't push them too hard, and they can go for a coffee whenever they like.'

'Can you take us to him?'

'Sure.' She stood up. 'Let's go and find him.'

And find him they did. Reading a paper in the break room.

'Brian, these gentlemen want to have a talk with you.' Heather looked at Miller. 'I'll be in my office if you need me.'

'Okay.' He looked at Hall. 'I'm DI Miller, this is DS Watt.'

'You're a bit old for a sergeant, aren't you?' Hall said, closing the paper and putting it aside. He nodded towards the door as Heather closed it. 'I don't fancy yours,' he said, but Watt ignored him.

They sat down opposite Hall.

'Brian, we want to know who the girl was that you had in the van,' Miller said.

Hall furrowed his brows. 'What girl? What van?'

Miller gave Watt a look before carrying on. 'Somebody saw you getting into a van with a girl who was murdered.'

Hall looked shocked. 'Me? No, sir, not me. He must have been mistaken.'

'What were you doing with a van?' Watt said.

'I drive a van for the warehouse, but we're not allowed to have people in them.'

'What do you deliver with the van?' Watt asked.

'They get food into the warehouse, and all sorts. Clothing, blankets, furniture. I deliver to the shelters, including this one. I alternate between here and there.'

'Are you often out with the van?'

'Quite a bit. Whenever they need me.'

'We ran your name through the system, Brian,' Miller said. 'We know you were put in borstal as a teenager for attempted rape.'

Hall's face darkened. 'She was a spoilt little daddy's girl who was a tease. When daddy found out, she said I tried it on with her. Her father was a lawyer, and they took his daughter's word for it. I never laid a hand on her.'

'If we find out you murdered that girl, you know what's going to happen to you, don't you?' Watt said.

'I didn't murder anybody.'

After a few minutes, they wrapped it up and left the room.

As they walked towards the lifts, Miller looked at Watt. 'Did you pick up on that?'

Watt nodded. 'I did.'

'We said somebody saw him, and he said, *He must have been mistaken.* How did he know the witness was a man?'

FOURTEEN

The snow forecast for Saturday morning hadn't materialised. Kim Smith drove the Audi into Kinnaird Shopping Centre on the east side of the city, past Craigmillar.

'I'll have to go pee before I go anywhere else,' Hazel said, patting the bump under her heavy winter coat.

'Don't worry, only another couple of months to go,' Kim said, getting out of the car. She walked round to help Hazel out. 'Then we can have a good old hooly. Suzie Campbell will be down with Percy Purcell before that, so she'll be up for it.'

'How's Percy doing?'

'He had to go back to Aberdeen to get his stuff together and move down here.'

Kim had only met Hazel at the start of the year when she had been working with Miller, but the two women soon became good friends. Now that DS Bruce Hagan had come back into her life, Hazel was happy but she would have been happier if he hadn't been attacked and left for dead. Hagan's recovery was going to take a long time.

'It's so good seeing you again, Kim,' Hazel said, as they went into the baby store. 'You know, before you came into our department, I was the only female.'

'I'm sure there would have been more. It's not every female who wants into CID, though God knows, you guys need them.'

The sky was grey and the wind cold, but the baby store was warm inside, Christmas carols were being piped in through the speakers, and even though it was reasonably early, because it was Christmastime, it was starting to get busy.

'What's Bruce doing today?' Kim said. 'He could have come with us.'

'Are you joking? I know he's been through a lot, Kim, but he's on a downward spiral. He wakes up in the middle of the night, screaming so loud Jane gets scared. In fact, she doesn't want to be alone with him, so she's with my mum, and he's going to a counselling session. Up at the Royal Scottish. He's been seeing a therapist there. Jill White, the woman we helped back in the summer.'

Kim nodded and looked grim. Jill had gone through her own version of hell. 'She's very professional. If anybody can help him, she can.'

After half an hour, they left and moved on to the big toy store.

'How are things with you and Frank?'

'Never better.' She smiled, and then stopped herself. 'I'm sorry.'

Hazel smiled and put her hand on Kim's arm. 'Don't be daft. There's nothing to be sorry about. I'm glad for you and Frank. He was at the lowest point for the longest time after he lost his wife, and you coming into his life was the best thing that could have happened to him. I'm so happy for you both. Even Jack has found somebody, and I'm pleased for him too.'

'You and Bruce will get things sorted. He's been through something that not a lot of people would come back from, and he'll get help from us all.'

'All you guys saved him that day. You gave him back to me and I'll never forget that.' She started to tear up so Kim gave her a hug.

'I'm always here for you.'

'I know. I'm just being a silly cow.' They looked at the dolls, and Kim picked one out to give to Jane, as well as one for her own daughter, Emma.

'Is there any sign of Frank putting a ring on your finger?'

'We said we'd see how it went after we moved in with each other. To be honest, I wanted to give him an out if he felt that he couldn't handle living with a little girl in the house, but he's taken to it like a duck to water. Emma loves him to bits, so you never know, he might get round to it.'

'I'm sure he doesn't want to lose you.'

'I'm not going to pressure him. Things are fine just now and I don't want to ruin it.'

'If he loves you, walking down the aisle will be the next step.'

'How about you and Bruce?'

'One step at a time, Kim. We only moved in together because he needed help adjusting. He's still got several surgeries to be done, but it's what's going on inside his mind that worries me. I don't think he'll ever get over that. So the last thing he's thinking of is marriage.'

They looked around a while longer before checking out.

'After the baby comes along, we should have a night out. Kate Murphy is always up for a night out. She's a good laugh, and since she moved up from London, she doesn't know many people in Edinburgh.'

'That sounds good. I like Kate.'

'Think about it.'

'I will. First of all though, I need to think about finding a bathroom.'

FIFTEEN

'Are you ready?' Frank Miller asked Kim, tapping his watch.

'It's a woman's prerogative to be late,' she said, smiling at him. 'One week before Christmas and you're getting all excited. Anxious to see what Santa's going to bring you?'

'Oh, I'm sure there'll be a jumper for Christmas in there somewhere. Personally, I think Santa should be fired; if he brings me another woollen jumper that will be the third time.'

'A man can't have too many, just remember that.'

'Oh, God, you've already bought me one, haven't you?'

Kim was standing in the middle of the living room, slipping her warm jacket on. 'Santa brings your gifts, I don't buy them.'

'Why I put up with your nonsense, I don't know.'

'Because you love me.' She walked over, put her arms around his neck, and kissed him.

'Who needs mistletoe?'

'As long as you don't go around kissing all the detective sergeants you work with.'

'There's only one female and she's heavily pregnant.' He pulled away from her for a moment. 'Which reminds me, did she say if she and Bruce are coming or not?'

'She was dog tired when we'd finished shopping, and she says Bruce doesn't go out anymore.'

'I haven't seen him in a few weeks. We should go round and spend time with them during Christmas.'

'Her mother's coming to stay for a couple of weeks. That'll be a great help.'

'They have us, too. And let's not forget what Bruce did for the department; he helped bring down a serial killer.'

'I'll never forget that, Frank.' She held onto him then, just needing to feel his arms around her.

She was the one who pulled away this time. 'Come on, boyfriend of mine, the Christmas party is in full swing.'

'It's eight o'clock, Kim. Full swing isn't what I'd call it.'

'Just because you're a night owl.'

'Although, you can bet your boots Andy is well pished by now.'

'Well, I'm not getting blootered. Somebody has to see you home safely.'

'It's so you can make sure no other female will take me away from you.'

'Like Fiona from the lab? If I see you anywhere near her with a piece of mistletoe...'

Miller could feel his face starting to go red. 'It was just two workmates having a laugh. Anyway, we should get going. I could murder a pint now. It's very rarely we all get to be together on a social occasion,' he said, changing the subject.

'Let's not waste any more time then.' She smiled at him.

They were just walking along the hallway to the front door when Kim's mobile phone rang. She answered it. 'Hello?'

Miller hoped it wasn't work. He'd been part of a team that had been on-call last Saturday night, but it had been quiet.

'Hold on, hold on, take it easy. Calm down, Vicky.' Kim turned round and mouthed, *I'm sorry.*

He just smiled at her, and went back to the living room to give her some privacy. He'd left the TV on, just for security, so he stood and watched a drama. Charlie, their cat, sat on the back of the settee, sleeping. Emma was over at Grandma and Grandpa's. Miller knew Jack adored Emma, and his mother would have loved her too, if she'd still been around and able to take a turn at babysitting.

He turned when Kim came back in. 'Everything okay?'

'No, it's Vicky.'

'Who's Vicky?'

'It's a woman I've been working with, Frank. She needs my help.'

'Tonight?'

'I'm afraid so.' Kim's mood had changed in an instant. 'I'm sorry, but I have to go now. I'll catch up with you.'

'Don't worry about it. I can come with you if you need my help.'

'No, you go. No point in us both missing out. Besides, I'll probably get to the dance later.'

'Do you want me to drive you to wherever you're going?'

'No, I'll be fine. Let me write down the address though, just in case.' She scribbled something down on a notepad and gave Miller the paper.

'If you need me, or all of us, just call me.'

'I will.'

'Can you tell me what it's about?'

'She's a victim, that's all I can say.'

Miller knew better than to ask more questions. Sometimes Kim had to work with victims under a cloak of secrecy.

'Then you go and help her. I'll either see you at the party later, or back here. Just keep in touch, and let me know you're safe.'

'I will. I love you, Frank Miller.'

'I love you too.'

Kim walked out of the apartment, and into the cold December night.

SIXTEEN

Podge walked round the corner, to where the lock-ups were. Stumpy owned one, which had originally belonged to his parents who'd left him the house and lock-up in their will.

His mother had told Stumpy she was glad he would be the one who was going to restore daddy's car. It was sitting in the lock-up, waiting for a bit of TLC, and Stumpy was going to bring it back to life.

This had been news to Stumpy.

The car was a scrapper. He'd seen it years before, when his father had taken him along for a squint. If you looked past the dirt and the rust, you could just about make out an Austin badge. 'She's a beauty, isn't she, son?' his father had said. 'I call her Katy.'

This was just as the dementia was starting to take hold. Maybe his father thought it was a Bentley and Katherine Hepburn was sitting in the driver's seat, waiting for him or something. Maybe waiting to drive him over to the other side.

'Stunning, Dad,' he'd said, not having the heart to tell his father if he sneezed hard enough, the car would be blown off its axles.

So, as soon as they'd nailed the coffin lid shut, Katy went on her holidays, to that big scrapyard in the sky.

When Ma learned he was going to the lock-up, she'd thought he was going to tinker with the old car. Now, the lock-up held nothing more exciting than an example of the staple diet of Britain's highways and byways; a white van.

'I have a nickname for it,' Stumpy had said, the first time Podge had clapped eyes on it.

'*The Yorkshire Ripper Express?*'

'No, the *Fanny Magnet.*'

Podge had shaken his head. 'Your idea of a fanny magnet is a little bit different from mine, I have to say. The only fanny who'd be interested in this thing would be a traffic warden.'

Now, Podge opened one of the barn doors of the lock-up. Stumpy was in the passenger seat. With the engine running.

'Are you trying to gas yourself, Stumpy?' Podge asked.

'I'm freezing.'

'You could have waited in the house. It's just round the fucking corner.'

'I couldn't wait to get going.'

Podge didn't know if the little man meant to the Pearly Gates or the work's dance. 'Just as well I'm here to keep you on the straight and narrow.'

'You're a good friend, I'll say that.'

'Don't get all weird on me now.' No matter how much he thought of Stumpy as a friend, he got a shiver down his back when the other man started getting sentimental.

Podge watched as Stumpy got out and he climbed into the driver's seat as Stumpy walked to the doors. He liked to drive, even though the van was Stumpy's.

'Are you looking forward to the Christmas night out tonight?' Stumpy asked him as he wound the driver's window down.

'Well, my social calendar is a bit full, but what the hell?' He looked at Stumpy as he opened the other door. 'Of course I'm looking forward to it. Vicky's not only going, she's going with *us*.'

'My thoughts exactly. I wasn't going to go, but Saturday night is drinking night for us, Podge.'

Podge couldn't care less about socialising, but he and Stumpy had agreed it would look better if they went, rather than their co-workers start to talk about them.

Don't want them to think I'm weird, Stumpy had said.

The ship sailed on that one a long time ago, my friend.

However, silver linings, and all that. Vicky had

asked them if they could stay over with her at her sister's house, and said to bring an overnight bag. They had readily agreed. Stumpy threw Podge's bag into the back of the van after he drove out, before closing the garage doors.

SEVENTEEN

Kim walked round to Cockburn Street and hopped into a taxi. It was only a five-minute ride down the road to the Dumbiedykes estate off Holyrood Road, but she flashed her identification card, told the driver she worked with the police, and promised him a good tip.

'No need,' he told her. 'I've had to call your guys a few times to empty out the drunks from the back of my cab. This is on me.'

'Thanks a lot.' She sat back and thought about the woman she was going to see, and in particular, the person who was terrorising her.

A few minutes later, they were there.

'Merry Christmas,' she said, to the driver.

The taxi rattled away. She pulled up the collar on her jacket, wishing she'd put on her work boots, instead of her dress boots. The snow made the place seem more festive, but there was still the air of untrustworthiness about it.

The flat she was looking for was on the second floor of a block near the main road.

It was deathly quiet – no doubt because many of the residents were in the town. Later on, the noise would start up. Her boots scuffed the concrete steps as she walked up the four, short flights of stairs.

Vicky was waiting at the door, like a little girl hiding from her.

'Oh, Kim, thank God you're here. He called and said he's going to kill me.'

'Nobody's going to touch you, Vicky.' She stepped into the hall and Vicky quickly shut the door behind her.

'I don't want you to think I'm overreacting, but he was very specific; he said he's going to slit my throat.' Vicky was pacing the living room, wringing her hands together. 'How the hell does he know I'm here? Or my phone number?'

'I don't know, but I'm going to find out.'

Vicky stopped so suddenly Kim almost bumped into her. 'I wish I hadn't pressed charges. ' She looked at her. 'You said I'd be safe, and it would be over after he was arrested.'

Kim looked at the small Christmas tree she'd helped Vicky dress, and the flashing coloured lights. Suddenly, things didn't look so festive.

She left the room for a moment, and called the

Police Intelligence Unit, explained the situation and waited for the return call. It came two minutes later. Kim went back into the living room.

'Your husband's still in Saughton. He hasn't used a phone, and as far as they know, he hasn't access to a mobile phone. Besides, he was in the communal area when you said you got the call.'

'Doesn't mean to say he didn't get somebody to call me.'

'I know. I'll do more digging.' She paused. 'Were you called on your house phone?'

'Yes,' she said.

'Let me see it.' Kim took the offered handset and scrolled through it until she found the number that had called last. She hit redial. The phone rang and rang but nobody answered. She took a note of the number.

'I'll have this number checked out, Vicky, otherwise my hands are tied. I want you to call me if he phones again, okay?'

She nodded, her face looking grim. 'At least the mortuary van won't have far to come.'

'Please don't talk like that,' Kim said. She knew, unfortunately, there were spouses who did indeed come back to exact revenge on the person they'd been physically abusing.

'Let me assume something for a moment; let's say it wasn't your ex. Do you know anybody who'd want to harm you? Or just scare you?'

'Like who?'

'Maybe somebody at work. Do you have a grievance with anybody?'

'No, we all get along in our department. In fact, it's the work's Christmas night out tonight, but I don't think I'll go now.'

'You should. Maybe see if somebody can pick you up.'

'That's already organised. Two friends from work are swinging by. I even suggested we stay over at my sister's house since she's away.'

'That's good. At least you'll be around people, and nobody will know you're going there.' She smiled and took Vicky's hand for a moment. 'You know, there are people who get kicks from calling random numbers and threatening people, or saying they're having an affair with the spouse. I think this was probably a prank.'

'Hold on though.' Vicky held up a finger and looked thoughtfully at Kim, and was about to say something then thought better of it. 'No, it couldn't be.'

'What, Vicky? Even if something seems impossible, just tell me.'

'Well, there's a worker at the shelter who's taken a shine to me. He's a nice guy, but I think he has a thing for me.'

'What's his name?'

'Brian Hall.'

'I'll have Frank check him out.'

'I'm relieved and angry all at once, Kim. I still think my ex is behind this.'

'There's a lot of sick people out there. You don't have to worry about your ex-husband though. He won't be going anywhere for a long time. Give me the address of your sister.'

Vicky wrote it down on a piece of paper and gave it to her. 'I'm sorry I ruined your night. Saturday night and you're here with me, instead of your boyfriend.'

'Don't worry about it. He's having fun with his friends and I'll catch up.'

Vicky hugged Kim. 'I need to hurry to get changed. Thank you so much for taking me seriously.'

'I'm always here for you, I told you that.'

'I feel so much better now.'

'Call me anytime, Vicky.'

'I will, thank you.'

'Now go and have a good time with your friends. Christmas only comes round once a year.'

Kim left the flat and walked down the road, hoping to find another taxi. Frank would be getting wired into the beer at the police club. She would be happy just being with him, even though she'd be drinking orange juice.

EIGHTEEN

'I wish I'd bought the old Ford Sierra I was originally after.'

Podge looked at him for a moment to see if he was joking as he parked in front of Vicky's place.

Stumpy shrugged his shoulders. 'It was bright red and had fluffy dice hanging from the mirror. Plus it was cheaper than this.' He looked at Podge. 'But there's room for a mattress in the back of this thing.' Stumpy rubbed his hands together, as if the manky old mattress in the back was actually going to get a workout.

The diesel clatter sounded deafening in the cold night air and Podge took his phone out and called Vicky. She sounded scared when she answered.

'We're downstairs in the...' he almost said *Fanny Magnet* but caught himself in time, 'Stumpy's van.'

'Thanks, Podge.'

He hung up. 'She'll be right down, so try and stay on your best behaviour.'

'She's a work colleague. Of course, I'm going to behave. I mean, it's not as if people get up to anything at a work's night out. Wink, wink.' He winked at Podge in the darkness.

I swear to Christ, if you wink at me while we're on the dance floor with women, I'll kill you where you fucking stand.

Podge saw Vicky walking down her pathway with a holdall. Stumpy got out, held the door for her and she climbed in after Stumpy threw the bag in the back.

'Hi, Podge.'

'Hey, Vicks,' Podge said, as she scooted along the bench seat. 'Ready to rock 'n' roll?'

'I almost didn't come tonight,' she said, as Stumpy climbed in and shut the door.

'Why? And miss a night out with the boys?'

'I got a threatening phone call.'

Podge felt himself going pale with anger. 'Who from?' he said, his voice battling against the noisy heater fan.

'I thought it was my ex. I thought he'd gotten out of prison, or he'd called or had somebody call. Whoever it was, he said he was going to slit my throat.'

Podge looked at Stumpy. This time, Stumpy didn't wink at him. 'Did you call the police?'

'Sort of. A woman came round. I've been working

with her. Kim Smith. She's the only one who took me seriously when my husband tried to kill me.'

'Who the hell would do something like that?' Stumpy said, gritting his teeth and shaking his head.

Podge wanted to say to her, *I hope it's not that nut job at the Washington.* Picturing Brian Hall in his mind, he reversed the van out.

'You're safe with us,' he said, simply. 'We'll look after you, Vicky.'

Vicky smiled at them. 'Thanks, boys. I'm feeling better already.'

NINETEEN

The Police Club on Queen Street used to house the headquarters for the local bus company, but they had amalgamated a few of their offices and the police had taken it over.

There were social evenings most weekends, in the suite through the back. Which was where the Christmas party was being held.

Kim checked her coat and walked through to the hall where the music was playing. Miller was dancing with a female sergeant from Leith CID and DI Matt Taylor was doing a slow dance in the middle of the others who were dancing at a more frenzied pace.

She went to the bar and Andy Watt slid up to her.

'I'll get this for you. I think your man is pre-occupied.' He smiled at her. 'I have to admit, I haven't seen him this happy for a long time. It's all thanks to you.'

'Andy, I do believe you're getting soft in your old age.'

'Less of the old.'

'Oh, yes, Frank mentioned you had met somebody new. Good for you.'

'Oh, trust him. I asked him to keep quiet about it.'

'It was just between us. I won't say anything.'

Watt paid for her orange juice. 'You're a cheap date,' he said, handing her the glass.

'Nothing cheap about me.' She took a sip. 'So tell me about your new lady.'

'I'm sure blabbermouth told you we met online. But it's a decent site, and she turned out to be a decent woman, not some catfish playing games. Win-win. I'm seeing her tonight after this.'

'I hope it all works out for you, Andy.'

'Thanks, Kim.' They clinked glasses.

The DJ told the crowd he was slowing the tempo, to give people a chance to catch their breath.

'Come on, let's make your boyfriend jealous.'

They put their drinks down and Kim laughed as Watt grabbed her hand and led her to the dance floor, where they slow danced to *Daydream Believer,* a song that wasn't too slow but slow enough to get the pulse rate down a bit.

She smiled over at Miller, who had gone back to the table with his friends. When the song ended, she and Watt got their drinks and joined the group.

'Orange juice, Kim?' DCI Paddy Gibb said when he saw her glass.

'I'm not much of a drinker, Paddy. After years of being on my own with Emma, I got used to staying sober.'

'I thought you would have had to be well blootered to have your hands on Watt.'

Watt raised his glass. 'Up yours.'

'What was that, Andy?' Gibb said, above the noise of the music.

'I said, cheers, boss.'

'All the best, son. I hope that woman you found on the internet doesn't turn out to be a bloke.' Gibb hiccupped and swallowed more lager.

Watt shook his head as the others looked at him. 'What? She's nice. We've been out a few times, and she's all woman.'

'You should have brought her along tonight,' Jimmy Gilmour said.

'And have all you wankers drool over her? No thanks.'

'Wankers?' Gibb said. 'We're your friends, you cheeky sod. Besides, I wouldn't fu—'

'Paddy!' Fiona from the lab shouted across at him from her own table. She stood up and smiled at Miller. 'There you are, Frank. I gave you my number and you never call. I hope you're not seeing somebody else behind my back.'

'Tell us more, Fiona,' Watt said. 'I'd pay money to see Kim scud Miller in front of us.'

'Thanks, Andy,' Miller said.

Fiona laughed. 'Don't worry, Kim knows I'm kidding.'

'Come on, Miller, time to shake those bones of yours.' Kim grabbed hold of Frank's hand and led him to the dance floor where *The Chicken Song* was just starting.

Miller groaned. 'In front of everybody? You're making me do this dance?'

Kim laughed. 'Of course I am. Move yourself, Miller. And don't get too drunk. I'm going to give you an early Christmas present.'

Miller made his chicken wings move faster.

TWENTY

Podge said he wanted to drive the van, not because he was a control freak, but because he didn't think Stumpy's driving skills were up to snuff. He thought they'd all die if Stumpy got behind the wheel.

'No, you deserve a drink, Stumps,' he'd said earlier. 'Just remember who we're with, and that I'm trying to impress her. And don't drink yourself under the table.'

'I remember, Podge; I can't get blootered.'

And so it was, Stumpy had too many to drive, but not enough that he'd be standing outside throwing up.

They'd kept their eyes on Vicky all night, and though their colleague had been up dancing with other men from the department, she never strayed far from her two friends.

Despite being a pain in the arse, Podge liked Stumpy a lot. His one true friend in life. And now the man who'd once described himself to a woman as *Stumpy-licious,* came bouncing off the dance floor as if he was having a seizure.

'You need to get up and shake your stuff, Podge,' he said, sitting down and scooping back his lager, his forehead gleaming. 'You need to get up and dance with Vicky. I swear to God she's going to kill me with those moves.'

'I prefer to be killed by a different set of moves, if you know what I mean.'

Stumpy laughed and drank more. 'Remember the first time Vicky ever came out drinking with us?'

'How could I forget? That little pub in Lothian Road had a dance floor, and you two were out of your skulls. And because she wanted to slow dance, you saw that as an invitation to put your hand on her arse.'

Stumpy grinned as if the village idiot had gotten loose. 'She didn't complain though.'

'She later told me she felt safe with us, even though you had a cheap feel.'

'Offence taken. There was nothing cheap about it,' Stumpy said, all mock indignation. 'I paid for the drinks *and* the taxi home.'

'Think of all the money you save by not putting your hand in your pocket every time we go out to the pub.'

'What? Fuck off.'

'Charming,' one of their female co-workers said, as

she passed. A young woman who neither of them had a snowball's chance in hell with.

'He made me say it,' he replied, but the woman wasn't listening. 'As I was saying, that first drinking sesh we had with her was magic. It would have stayed that way if her wanker of a husband hadn't started throwing her about.'

Podge looked troubled for a moment.

'Why the long face, Podgy boy?'

'Just thinking, Stumps.' He looked his friend in the eyes. 'I think Vicky's in this position because of me.'

'What position?'

Podge shook his head. 'Attention span of a fucking goldfish, that's you. 'This,' he waved his hand in a circular motion, '*position* we're in. With her husband being in prison and now he's threatening her.'

'First of all, you can't blame yourself. And secondly, we don't know for a fact it was him who called her.'

'Vicky's husband's in prison because of me.'

'How come?'

'You know, after that first Friday night, the three of us used to go out drinking after work every Friday?'

Stumpy nodded his head up and down like a bobble-head.

'Well, one night after we were drinking, and you'd gone home early because you felt the shits coming on or something—'

'I was actually meeting a girl that night, if you remember correctly,' Stumpy interrupted.

'Yeah, Pam and her five sisters,' Podge said, holding up a hand and doing *jazz hands* with it. 'Anyway, I was walking Vicky home, and who should pull up in his car but Mr Vicky. He got out and gave her a right dressing down in the street. Pointed his finger at me and said he wasn't finished with me. But he got in the car and drove away with her, and I never thought any more about it. Until one night, I was coming out of the boozer, and who should be waiting there with his mate, but the Neanderthal himself. Reminded me he hadn't forgotten about me.

'Unfortunately for him, he fights like a fairy. I skelped his fucking jaw and knocked him on his arse. Gave his pal a bloody good belting as well, and he dragged Mr Vicky away, both of them bleeding and groaning. I never heard from him again, but it wasn't long after that, Vicky started coming in with a black eye.'

'It's not your fault he's a nut job.'

'I just wish I hadn't encouraged her to come out with us. Maybe he would've left her alone.'

'Jesus Christ, Podge, you know deep down as well as I do, he's a wife beater, and he just needed an excuse to belt her. He saw it, and went for it. We don't know he hadn't done it to her before, just because we didn't see it.'

Podge looked impressed. 'You're not as daft as you

look. You know, every time you make sense, an angel gets its wings.'

Stumpy was still thinking about it when Podge hit the dance floor with Vicky. He didn't put his hand on her arse.

TWENTY-ONE

Jesus, all those people going out to their Christmas parties on a Saturday night, making it harder to get a taxi. Cindy was mightily pissed off as she trudged the wet, slippery pavement along Warriston Road.

It had been a great night out, and she was glad she'd gone. Earlier in the week, she'd promised herself, no matter how much her friend convinced her to go, she'd stay in and watch TV. Maybe watch one of those shows she liked to record. The true-life crime dramas where the wife murders the husband. Some of those women were just stupid, and they would have gotten away with it if they'd just screwed the nut a little bit tighter.

She would have killed *her* ex if she'd known she could get away with it.

Her friend had nagged and nagged until she'd

promised she'd go. And Cindy was glad she'd gone. It was a great night out. Except for this part.

Up past the DIY store and the houses, the cemetery on the other side of the high wall, the same cemetery where several murders had taken place, but now, the only dead people in there had a headstone above them.

She headed up the road, the walkway, which was once a railway line, on her left, next to the cemetery wall. The dividing line between the dead and the living. A wind kicked up, blowing snow from the trees that lined the street. She liked the snow, but not when she had to walk in it.

She continued over the pedestrian bridge that crossed over the walkway farther up the road, and continued along Warriston Road. This part ran alongside the high wall that kept the cemetery at bay. Past the gate that led into the corporation allotments opposite the cemetery.

A white van sat at the side of the road farther up, its cab empty. There hadn't been any cars along this way since she'd started walking. This was what her friend had called a "dead" street, and he hadn't meant because there were hundreds of bodies just over the wall, but because there were no houses here. Nobody to see you being mugged, she'd warned.

Well, she'd made it this far and was nearly home, and there was nothing parked here except this scabby old van. With nobody in it. She hurried past, not giving it a second glance.

TWENTY-TWO

I follow Cindy after waiting for her to come out of the nightclub. She gets on a bus after hanging about for a taxi and not getting one.

When I see her walking down Logie Green Road, I know there's little chance of her getting a taxi and she'll probably just be walking home. It's not far from her house anyway. So I drive on and wait.

Then I see her coming along Warriston Road, at the side of the cemetery. Where the side gate is.

As she comes towards me, I'm waiting in the back despite the cold, but I have the back door open a crack, and it isn't long until she appears. As she passes by, I slip out, slip the sack over her head, and loop the rope over it, pulling it tight but not too tight. I then haul her into the back of the van and lock it.

The fucking bitch could scream, that was for sure.

I'd opened the cemetery gates a little after I parked,

so now I drive in after getting Cindy in the back. I close them again so no nosy copper will see them open. I take a brush and quickly obliterate the tyre marks and then I drive farther in. I'm careful not to give it too much gas in case it slides off the road and hits a gravestone and I get stuck. Try and explain that away!

As it is, the snow has thinned down a lot and the main drive is pretty clear. I have my headlights on, the beams bouncing off the snow, making it look like I'm on another planet.

Being surrounded by death in the dark doesn't scare me. If anybody is in here now, they should be scared of me!

Farther down the track, I pull the van into the side. It's almost like a Winter Wonderland here, the trees and grass still covered in snow. Looking around, none of the houses on the other side of the wall can be seen, and if you use your imagination, you might think you're in Alaska, or any other far-flung destination, instead of an old cemetery in the middle of Edinburgh.

I turn the engine off and get out of the van. Slam the door and walk away. Stand and look at my watch, and wonder how long it will take.

TWENTY-THREE

'I feel like I'm spoiling your night, Podge,' Vicky said, as they danced slowly in a circle.

Podge held her, maybe a little closer than he should, but it had been such a long time since he'd held a woman in his arms. Chris De Burgh was singing *Lady in Red* and just for that moment in time, Vicky was his. He'd been quite happy when Stumpy had been up on the dance floor giving it yahoo to Jive Bunny and Roy Wood, but now it was his turn after the DJ had turned it down a notch. If a Kenny G song came on; he wouldn't be able to contain himself.

'I can't think of anywhere I'd rather be right now, Vicky. We've always got along; from the moment you came to work at social services.'

'I know, Podge.' Vicky looked into his eyes as they slowly made their way round the dance floor. 'I've always wanted to ask you how you got the nickname *Podge?*'

'Let's just say, I wasn't always this thin. I was a lot heavier when I was at school, and somebody called me *Podge* and it stuck. Only my friends call me that.'

'And I'm your friend.' She smiled at him. 'You don't think Stumpy's going to get jealous, do you? Seeing us dance this close?'

Podge laughed quietly. 'Have a look for yourself.'

Vicky looked over his shoulder and saw Stumpy slow dancing with a divorcee, their faces seemingly glued together. She looked back at him. 'I think he's struck lucky tonight.'

'Not tonight. We're coming home with you, remember? Two knights in shining armour.'

Vicky pulled back for a moment. 'There I go, spoiling your fun again. Look around you, Podge; you could have any woman in here. You're a good-looking bloke, you just have to put yourself out there a bit.'

'I'm not going anywhere but back to your place. If you still want us to, that is. God, the last thing I want is for you to think I'm going to be trying something funny.'

'Oh, I want you to come home with me, Podge, more than anything. And you're one of God's own gentlemen. I don't think I've ever felt safer with a man. You and Stumpy are my two best friends.'

'You know you can call me anytime, and we can

have a few beers or go and see a film or something. I've not been out with many women since my divorce.'

'Things will be easier when my own divorce is finalised,' she said as the song ended. 'Would it be remiss of me if I kissed you?'

'Not at all.' Podge said, pressing his lips against hers as the dance floor became even darker.

Songbird started playing.

Thank you, God, Podge thought, and pulled Vicky in closer.

TWENTY-FOUR

I wait patiently in the dark, standing round the side of the van with the shovel I've brought. I've taken her handbag so she doesn't have her mobile phone to call for help. I hear her banging about in the van, trying to get the rope off. It takes her longer than I thought it would. I've left it loose enough for her to escape but still she's struggling with it.

God, I can feel the adrenaline run through me in anticipation. Just the thought of what I'm going to do to her makes me hyper.

Then the back doors open. I watch as she scoots out, legs first, and then stands up.

I silently step round from the side of the van with the shovel raised and bring it round in a perfect arc. The metal of the head smacks her right in the face. Blood flies out in a spray, tainting the freshly fallen snow with its vibrant colour. She screams and falls back into the snow at the side of the track.

Then I stand looking down at her. 'Hello, Cindy,' I say, adding to her confusion.

'Please don't hurt me,' she says, reaching out a hand to ward off further attack. She puts a hand to her nose and feels the warm blood pouring out.

'Already have,' I say.

'Please. Who are you? I'll do whatever you want, just let me go.' Her voice sounds as if she's choking, as the blood starts coursing down her throat.

'That's very kind of you,' I say, bending over so I'm closer to her, 'but I'm going to take a pass on that.' I straighten back up.

Shock hits her, making her feel even colder. The sky is black and clear, but the snow fills all the dark corners, making everything seem lighter and less scary.

Except she's more afraid than she's ever been in her life.

'We're going to play a game,' I say.

Cindy looks at me. Wants to ask me what sort of game, but knows she's going to find out soon enough.

'Please, I don't want to play any game. Just let me go and I won't say anything.'

'If you want to go home, you have to earn your release. You have to play the game... and win.'

Cindy struggles onto her side, more blood dripping into the snow. Onto her hands and knees. Maybe she thinks if she humours me, I'll let her go.

'Okay. I'll play. What do you want me to do?' she asks, as she finally manages to get to her feet.

My face gets closer to hers, and I say one word:

'Run.'

TWENTY-FIVE

The DJ had slowed the music and Kim kissed Miller while it was still dark. Then they left the dance floor for another drink. 'I'm going to give my friend a call, the one I had to go and see earlier,' Kim said.

'Okay,' Miller said, as Watt came across with more drinks.

'Going away to call a friend, eh? Next thing you'll be telling Frank it's not him, it's you.'

'Thanks, Andy. I was going to tell Frank that you and I have been secretly dating, but you've let the cat out of the bag.'

'I wish.' He sat down and looked at Miller. 'Not that I would, boss.'

'Of course not, Andy. Cheers.'

Kim walked through to the lobby and climbed up to the first landing where it was quieter. She stopped and took her phone out.

'Hello, Vicky? It's Kim. I'm just calling to see if everything's alright?'

'Hi, Kim. Everything's fine. I'm actually having a good time with my friends.'

'No hassle or phone calls?'

'Nothing. As I said, I'm staying at my sister's place and my friends will be staying over with me. I'll be fine. Thanks for your help tonight.'

'That's what I'm here for. If you need me again, don't hesitate to call.'

'I won't. Enjoy the rest of your night.'

'Bye, Vicky.'

Kim hung up and went back to join Miller.

'Everything okay?' he asked her.

'It's fine.' She leaned in closer as the music started up again. Watt had gone off in search of a dance partner. 'This woman received a death threat on the phone. Her husband is in prison, and as far as we can tell, he wasn't near a phone when she got the call. She did tell me about a man at Washington House who's taking an interest in her.'

'Washington House?'

'Yes. She's an administrator in social services who has to go there regularly.'

Miller furrowed his brow, his interest piqued. 'Do you know his name, by any chance?'

'His name's Brian Hall.'

Miller sat back in his chair.

'Do you know him?' Kim asked.

'Yes I do. We spoke to him. Andy and I were interviewing somebody who thinks Hall murdered the girl we found on Portobello beach.'

TWENTY-SIX

Run, *I'd said, and that's exactly what she's doing. As best she can in high heels, anyway. Following the roadway at first,* Cindy *suddenly darts off to one side, her feet sinking through the deeper snow, slowing her down.*

I can almost see her thinking: What's the lesser of two evils, sticking to the road and moving faster, or going this way and slowing myself down?

Either way, she must know it won't be long before I start chasing her.

Her breath blows out of her mouth like a dragon's fire, and her breathing becomes laboured the more she runs. Although out of breath, she's making good time.

I move silently away and watch her from my vantage point. I've taken a different direction and cut her off. She climbs the snow-covered hill, as the cemetery ascends from the lower part. The smooth soles of her shoes slide on the snow as her weight compresses it, but she digs in as hard as she can.

She's almost at the top when she decides to turn and look, maybe to see if I'm right there, about to suddenly grab her ankle and yank.

I'm not there.

She thinks she's lost me. Beaten all the odds and actually outrun me. She turns back at the crest of the hill and looks up at the huge monolith somebody's ego had paid for when they died, and she can actually see the stars in the dark, clear sky...

'Well, you took your time, Cindy,' I say, stepping out from behind the monolith. I'm holding the shovel in one hand.

She screams as loud as she can and starts sliding back down the hill, feeling the snow slide up her party dress. 'Get away from me, you freak!'

'Now, now, that's hardly the Christmas spirit.'

Down the bottom of the hill, momentum keeps her going, and by God's own intervention, she finds herself still on her feet. She can't run any more.

She turns round and watches as I casually wander down the hill through the deep snow, following the snail trail she's left. My boots sink into the deep drifts as I progress ever closer to her.

'I'm coming for you, Cindy. It's just you and me now. Nobody around to save you.' I have the shovel slung over my shoulder as if I'm off to work somewhere.

This seems to kickstart something in her brain. She takes her shoes off and starts running in earnest.

I reach the bottom of the hill and stand staring at her back. God, this is fun.

I disappear from view.

She walks along the roadway and turns at the corner of the cemetery, knowing it isn't far to the gate now. Blood is still running down her face despite her best efforts to stop it.

I jump out at her from behind a gravestone, and she screams, 'You demented bastard.'

'You forgot your bag,' I say, and throw it into a snow bank.

She bends to get it. As she stands up, her eyes widen as she sees my gloved hand coming towards her face. She thinks I'm going to punch her but she doesn't see the knife with its slim blade sticking out between my fingers. It slides through her eyeball with little resistance, and keeps on going, into her brain. I step aside as the blood spurts from the wound, the destructed eye now filling with blood.

I leave the knife where it is and watch her fall backwards. Then I grab her by the legs, and drag her back to where the grave for Monday's funeral has been dug. The obituary said the funeral, to which all family and friends are invited to attend, will be happening at ten o'clock.

And pretty soon after they turn up, officers from Police Edinburgh will surely put in an appearance.

TWENTY-SEVEN

'Well, best of luck, Andy,' Miller said, as they made their way out the front door of the club. A shower of snow had fallen, sprinkling the pavements. They could see their breath in the cold night air.

'I won't need luck, boss. I just have this animal charm about me.'

'As long as you have your breath spray about you, you'll be fine.'

'Locked and loaded.' He brought out his little can of Gold Spot and fired a couple of shots into his mouth.

They watched as a BMW glided into the side of the road and the driver honked the horn. Watt waved to the woman who had leaned over so she could see them. He turned to Miller and Kim. 'Oh, did I not mention she was minted?' He laughed, walked down the steps, and got into the car.

'No, that's okay, we don't want a lift,' Miller said, to the retreating taillights.

Kim laughed as she pulled her scarf farther up her neck and looped her arm through his. 'Where did Andy find a woman with money?'

'*Like it rough dot com.*'

'You're bad.'

'I hope she treats him right. Andy's a good guy.'

'I know.'

Miller's mind started to wander. He found it hard to turn off being a detective, even for just a few minutes.

'You're thinking about that girl again, aren't you?' Kim said, as they started strolling east along Queen Street, arm in arm It was so cold now, and groups of revellers were milling about, not nearly finished with their carousing.

'I am.' They turned into North St David Street, heading through St Andrew Square on their way home. 'It's hard not to, Kim. She looks like she's a teenager, barely starting out in the world, then she gets murdered.'

'We're going to get the bastard who did this, Frank.'

'I can't help taking things personally when somebody takes advantage of another human being.' He looked at her. 'I just wish I could look into his eyes and ask him why.'

'I've a feeling you'll get the chance. We're all

working hard on it. Just because it's only a week until Christmas, doesn't mean we'll slack off.'

'I know we won't. I even felt guilty about coming to this do tonight. I feel we should all be out looking for her killer.'

'There are times when you just have to take a deep breath. Like a long-distance swimmer; you can only hold your breath for so long. Then you go at it with renewed vigour.'

He squeezed her hand tighter. 'I know this is a once a year affair. And you're right, come Monday morning, we'll be steaming ahead like a train. But it doesn't stop me feeling sad and angry that there's a young girl lying on a steel tray in a fridge in the mortuary.'

'I know.' She pulled him closer. 'Princes Street always looks magical at this time of year, don't you think?'

'I love it. I don't think I could work anywhere else in the world.'

They walked round into the North Bridge. Almost home. Unlike a young girl who would never be celebrating Christmas again.

TWENTY-EIGHT

Podge knew he was in love. It was real this time. Not like schoolboy love, a crush a teenager might have on a girl sitting opposite him in English.

He knew he was falling in love with Vicky. He was quite happy to be her friend, because that way, he could spend time in her company without driving her away. But when she'd kissed him on the dance floor earlier, he knew she felt the same way about him.

Her being married was just a little hiccup that would soon be resolved. *Then what, Podge?* What was he going to do then? What did he have to offer her?

Well, let's see: you own your own home (And *it wasn't in a shitty part of the city, thank you very much); you have a decent job with prospects; he was dashingly handsome. What was not to like?*

Maybe he could get together with her, if he played

his cards right. After being on his own for years, maybe they did have a future together.

First, though, they had to get through this weekend.

'Swanky!' Stumpy said from the passenger seat, as Podge fought with the steering wheel on the slick road. Too much to ask the gritters to come down these side streets, he thought.

They were in Orchard Brae Avenue. Her sister had bought the house a few months ago, liking its central location.

'This is a nice area,' Vicky said, looking around at the townhouses. 'My sister said I could stay here if I wanted to save me coming round to water the plants and check on the place. I thought it might not be a bad idea.' She looked at Podge, the meat in the *Podge and Stumpy sandwich* again. 'And I'm glad I asked you two to stay with me.'

'Well, now you have Batman and Robin to look after you.' *Or Laurel and Hardy, depending which side of the fence you were on.*

'Your sister must have money dripping out of her—'

'Stumps!' Podge shouted. 'Manners. We have a lady in here.'

Stumpy grinned, and Podge could see a line of sweat on his friend's brow, hoping to God it was because of the heater vent and that he wasn't playing pocket golf again.

'Vicky's a mate, she doesn't mind,' Stumpy said.

'Well, *I* do.'

Stumpy kept on grinning, and just for a moment, Podge felt like he and Vicky were a happy couple, taking their older, special needs son out for his first time in the snow. Vicky, sitting in the dark of the van and staring straight ahead, put her right hand on Podge's thigh in a silent *Thank you.*

Trying to keep the van out of the front gardens of the houses on the other side of the street, he felt the back end sliding back and forth like a drunken sailor and was sweating just as much as Stumpy by the time they pulled up at the townhouse. He pulled the van into the driveway in front of the garage.

Podge put on a posh accent. 'Madam, shall I put the carriage away for the evening?'

Vicky laughed.' No, James, you may keep her here. I may require a ride later on.'

Jesus, Podge thought, and laughed at her innuendo. He looked over at Stumpy, thinking he was going to say, *Me too!*

Podge turned the engine off and they all got out, Stumpy going round to the back of the van and opening one of the doors while Vicky went to the townhouse. He picked up his own bag and Vicky's, while Podge came round and grabbed his own.

'Guess what, Podgy boy?'

'You found out your dad was a leprechaun.'

'Apart from that.'

'I dunno, Stumps. Don't keep me in suspense.'

'I got that girl's number tonight.'

'What girl?'

'The one from accounts. She gave me her number.'

'What is it? six six six?'

'No, it's a Dalkeith number.'

Podge looked at him. 'Are you going to call her?' he said, closing the back door. Vicky at the front door, fiddling with the key.

'Of course I'm going to call her. She said she's been watching me but didn't know how to ask me out.'

'She *was* conscious when she was saying this? I mean, she wasn't lying down, pished out of her skull and you translated her moans as *Stumpy I want to have your children?*'

Stumpy laughed. 'No, Mister Smart-arse. She only had a few. She gave me her number quite willingly.'

'Good for you. I hope she's not going to string you along.' *I hope she doesn't have six kids and needs you to feed them when she jacks her job in.*

'I'm a big boy, Podge. I know when a girl wants to sample some of the *all-you-can-eat-Stumpy.*'

'Good God, I wouldn't lead with that if she actually meets you for a drink.'

'One night in *Stumpyland* will have her coming back for more, let me tell you.'

Podge shook his head. 'What do you dream of at night, my poor, wee lad?'

'Not you, that's for sure.'

'Got it,' Vicky said, opening the door and dealing

114

with the alarm, appreciating the warmth of the central heating. 'Welcome to my sister's home,' she said, switching on a light.

'Lead the way to the drinks cabinet, Vicks,' Stumpy said, stepping over the threshold as Vicky closed the door behind them. They went upstairs to the next level.

'This is a nice place your sister has here,' Stumpy said, standing in the middle of the living room.

'Uh, oh, better hide the silverware, Stumpy's in town,' Podge said.

'Lock up your daughters, you mean,' Stumpy said, surveying the room.

'The living room, kitchen, and a toilet are on this level, while the bedrooms are upstairs,' Vicky said.

'After you,' Podge said.

They were each shown a room, and told the main bathroom was just down the hall. Vicky would take the master, which had its own bathroom.

'Do you want a drink? There's beer in the fridge,' Vicky asked.

'I think we should call it a night,' Podge said. 'Don't you agree, Stumps?'

'I suppose so.' He yawned. 'Don't you worry about a thing, Vicky. I've got this with me.' He opened his bag and pulled out a small baseball bat.

'What's that?' Podge said, taking a hold of it. '*Souvenir of Spain.*'

'If anybody comes near us, he'll get this.'

'Just seeing you storming out in your vest and skids will make anybody run, Stumps. You won't even have to wave that wee thing about.'

Stumpy put the bat away in his bag. 'It's not how small it is, it's how you use it. *As I'm sure Vicky's about to find out,*' he said, almost under his breath.

Podge gave him a look and hoped Vicky hadn't heard him. 'Well, goodnight, now. Sleep tight. And if you die in your sleep, may the Lord take your soul.' *Please God.*

'I'll see you both in the morning. Oh, and Podge? I take my eggs fried and my bacon crispy.'

'Good to know. If you give me her number, I'll be sure to call that girl in Dalkeith before you take her out.'

Stumpy laughed as he closed his bedroom door, leaving Vicky and Podge standing alone in the hallway.

'I'm glad we all decided to go along to the Christmas night out,' Vicky said.

'Me too.'

'Podge, I think I'm falling for you. I mean, I know I'm still married, but I was never happy. When you, Stumpy and me went out drinking, I felt I was with the man I was meant to be with. And I don't want you to think I was just with you to feel secure. I started falling in love with you.'

'I'm falling for you too.'

She gazed into his eyes and rubbed a hand through his hair. 'Spend the night with me, Podge.'

'It would be unfair of me to take advantage of the situation. I want to be with you, but I want to do it right. To woo you, to romance you, not to rush into anything.'

'I haven't had a lot to drink. You wouldn't be taking advantage of me, Podge. I've known you for a long time, and now we have this chance to be together. I want you, and I want you now.'

And with that, Podge gave in.

TWENTY-NINE

I drive twice round the estate, and don't spot their van. So they've dropped her off and left her alone, is my first thought.

I smile to myself in the darkness. Now all I have to do is finish this one off and my Saturday night out will be complete.

I park the van, looking around to make sure there are no drunks piling out of a fast black. I close the van door and make my way up to the building, quietly opening the door and walking up to her landing. This is where time is of the essence. I pull out the mini-crow-bar, a tool that could have been made especially for housebreakers, and jam it into her front door. I know I have to get right in and do the business before she has a chance to grab her phone.

The door jamb splinters. It's cheap and nasty, and gives little resistance. I'm through the doorway in the blink of an eye, pushing it closed. The flat is in darkness. Good, it means she's most likely in bed. I have to move fast; if I've woken her, she could be calling the police.

I go for what I think is a bedroom, but the bed is empty. Same with the other one. She isn't in any of the rooms. Where the hell is she? Late home from the party?

I can't afford to wait for her to come home. Some-body might see the broken door and call the police. I go round opening the drawers in her room and emptying them quietly. I know it's her room because all her stuff is in here. I'll make it look like a burglary. Then I go into her toilet. Take out the piece of tape that has been carefully stuck on the piece of plastic, and gently press it onto the flush handle on the cistern. I look around, then leave. I'll get her later. After all, I know where she works.

I know where they all work.

THIRTY

Frank Miller was fully refreshed, after sobering up on Sunday. Monday morning brought with it a new headache, in the form of the woman who was lying dead in the old cemetery, with a knife sticking out of her skull.

'The council blokes found her,' DS Andy Watt informed Kim. 'They were pulling back the boards for a funeral when they saw her lying behind a gravestone.'

'Jesus, poor cow,' Kim said as Miller came across.

'We're running a background check on those guys, and doing a follow-up on their alibis.' He looked over at Jake Dagger, who was standing near the SOCOs. 'Doc over there, reckons sometime on Saturday night into early Sunday, and the gravediggers say they were at a party.'

'Do we have an ID?' Kim asked.

'Cindy Stevenson. Lives just along the road there, according to her driving licence. Her bag is here, with all her belongings in it.'

Dagger approached. 'I won't know for sure until I cut her open, but it's looking as if the knife rammed into her eye killed her. Or the blunt force trauma, whichever came first. Something with a flat surface. Whatever it was, it looks as if her eye socket's shattered and her nose is badly broken.'

'Like a piece of wood or something?' Miller said.

'I'd say more like a shovel. Double-check the alibis for those gravediggers.'

Miller looked at them. 'Maggie Parks is going through their van now. Doesn't mean to say they didn't kill her with another shovel and brought a different one to work today.'

Inspector Maggie Parks was in charge of the Identity Branch and was the head SOCO.

'What are your thoughts on this, boss?' Watt said. He still looked hungover from Saturday night.

'I think they'd be stupid to kill her and leave her out here where she'd be found today. They're pulling a backhoe behind their truck, so why not dig a hole, and bury her in the older part of the cemetery, where she wouldn't be found?'

Miller looked at the blood on the snow around the woman's head. Whoever did this shouldn't be allowed to breathe God's sweet air, he thought.

'Right, Andy, you're with me. I want to go and see

if we can rustle up a next-of-kin. Maggie, do you have the keys for Cindy's house?'

'Yes, I have them.'

'Can you spare a couple of members of your team to come with me for a quick scout?'

'Sure.' She issued instructions for two of her senior team members to take one of the vans and go with Miller.

'Kim, you supervise here.' Miller left in his car with Watt, grateful to be back in the warmth. The snow had held off, but more was forecast. They'd been getting belted with it recently, and there was no sign of it letting up.

The house where Cindy lived was part of a two-up, two-down affair, near the end of the road, just off Ferry Road. There was no answer from her door and a neighbour answered from the flat opposite.

'Police,' Miller said, introducing himself. 'Can you tell me who lives here?'

'Cindy Stevenson. Why, what's wrong?'

'We're just making enquiries. Does she live with anybody?'

The older woman pulled her cardigan tighter round her front. 'No, she got divorced a few years back and she told me they haven't spoken in years.'

'Do you know his name?'

'She never said. She moved here after the divorce and went back to using her maiden name. She just told me they were never close. She was drunk at the time,

122

and started going on about something or other. I didn't socialise with her at all.'

'You've been very helpful.'

They waited for the SOCOs to come up the stairs and Miller unlocked the door and let them in. They followed, putting on overshoes.

After half an hour, they'd found nothing that might indicate a next-of-kin. No address for her ex-husband or anybody else. Miller left the keys with the SOCOs.

Back in the car, he cranked the heat up. 'It doesn't get us very far, Andy.'

'We're going to have to keep her name out of the papers, until we try and track family down.'

'That's going to be hard.' Before he pulled away, he answered a call from Kim. After a few minutes, he hung up.

'The body's been moved now. We're going back to the station.'

'Okay.'

'So spill the beans, Andy,' Miller said, as they stopped at a traffic light.

'What you on about, boss?'

'Don't be acting all innocent now. You tell me Jean's minted just before she whisks you away in her Beemer on Saturday night and you think you're going to keep that to yourself?'

Watt sat looking as if he was the cat who just had the last drop of milk in the house. 'I was up front with her from the beginning, and she knows I'm a copper, and still she wants to go out with me.'

'So what does she do with herself?'

'She's a businesswoman. That's all she would say for now.'

'You're going to do something daft and look her up on our database, aren't you?'

'No, I'm not actually, thank you. I intend to make a go of this with her, if that's what she wants. I don't want to risk anything.'

'Good for you,' he said, pulling away from the lights.

Fifteen minutes later, Miller made it through the heavy traffic to the station.

There were several investigation suites on the upper level, and the one Miller worked out of had already been set up for the murder of the teenage girl last week. All the drinking and hilarity from Saturday had been forgotten. Now it was business as usual.

DCI Paddy Gibb stood in front of the whiteboard. 'Right, everybody, I know we all had a good time at the weekend, and Andy slinked off early to go somewhere, but time to get back to business.'

Andy Watt sat with raised eyebrows. 'As much as I wanted to go pub crawling with you afterwards, boss, I was seeing a lady.'

'Well make sure you let all the air out of her before you have company round,' Gibb said. After the laughter died down, he got serious. 'Right, team. I have an identification for you; Sabrina Hailes, aged fifteen, a runaway from Birmingham. Her name is on the database down there, and it was flagged, so they gave us a call. Get this though; nobody wants to come up here to identify her.'

'So we're assuming she was sleeping rough?' Watt said.

'We were thinking along those lines, after we didn't get any info from around here. She didn't have any identification on her, and nobody had reported her missing, so we were starting to cast the net wider. However, I had Jake Dagger on the phone late Friday. He said if she *was* living on the streets, she was eating very well. She had steak in her stomach and no sign of malnutrition. In fact, she was very clean and her hair had been washed recently.'

Gibb walked over to a large computer monitor and hit the spacebar, bringing it to life. The CCTV picture of a masked robber in a jewellery store appeared. 'We need to know where she got those earrings. They were definitely the pair stolen in this robbery. We can't rule out this being her. I had an expert look at it, and he said, given her measurements and considering the boots the robber was wearing, it *could* be her. If somebody else turned this place over, those earrings followed a route between being taken out of that cabinet and being found on the corpse. We need to follow that trail.'

Miller said, 'We had a witness come in and give us

a name, a man who was seen with her, but it didn't pan out. The man is a maintenance worker at Washington House homeless shelter. We're checking the CCTV from buses that went by at the time of the robbery, and we've also contacted taxi companies to see if any drivers were in that area at that time. So far, we've hit a dead end.'

'We're going to be checking shelters, see if anybody recognises her,' Gibb said. 'Take a copy of her mortuary photo. If you get to any place and they won't let you search, I'll get onto Norma Banks and she can rustle up a judge to give us a search warrant. Frank, you take Andy with you. Start with the shelter in Leith. The rest of you, I have your assignments on the desk over there. We'll meet back here, and hopefully we'll have a report from the mortuary regarding the woman who was found in the cemetery this morning.'

They disbanded and Miller headed downstairs with Watt to their pool car.

THIRTY-ONE

'We're a charity,' Len McLennan said, as he showed Miller and Watt along to the offices. 'Everything is paid for through donations. We're doing really well after the big cock-up of 2008.'

Home from Home was the homeless charity that owned Washington House. They were at the warehouse where it stored donated food and furnishings.

They reached the small office at the end of a short corridor. Inside, McLennan slumped into a chair and let out a breath, as if he'd been run off his feet all morning.

'I'd like you to look at this photograph and see if you recognise the young woman in it.' No point in telling him she was only a young girl.

The manager took it and studied it for a moment. 'She's dead, isn't she?'

'I'm afraid she is, yes.'

He looked at the photo again. 'I can't say I recognise her, but then again, have you seen the mortuary photos of Marilyn Monroe? Looks nothing like her. So, my first guess is, no, I don't recognise her. Do you know for a fact she was at the home sometime?'

'No, we're not sure where she was living,' Watt said.

'I'm guessing she was a runaway, considering you're here asking me, and we only take in under eighteens. But to be honest, I'm rarely up at the home.'

'Why only youngsters?' Miller said.

'There are various charities throughout the city who deal with older kids and adults.'

'And somebody started this charity for younger kids?'

McLennan nodded. 'A woman set up *Home from Home*. She had a fifteen-year-old daughter who ran away to London and got in with the wrong crowd. She got pregnant. Twice. Then she came home to her mother. So this woman wanted to set up something here, so if any young person ran away from home, they'd have a safe haven.' He looked at both detectives. 'There are a lot of scumbags out there who'll exploit those poor kids.'

Andy Watt nodded in agreement. 'Do any of your drivers give them a lift from the shelter? Or interact with them at all?'

'First of all, if I catch any of them giving a lift to somebody, I'll can his fucking arse out the door. Our insurance would go through the roof if somebody was in that van and it got into an accident and they were hurt.

'And yes, they interact with the homeless people. Most of them do double duty at something.'

'Like Brian Hall,' Watt said.

'Yeah, like him. He drives and he's a maintenance worker. We keep him on his toes.'

'Could he have given this girl a lift?' Miller asked.

'Anything's possible. They look out for young people who seem vulnerable, and if they see somebody, they're supposed to call a social worker.'

'So, he could have been out with the van, saw this girl, and interacted with her?'

'Could have. He could see somebody sitting in a doorway, and approach them with one of our business cards. They can give us a call or they can call social services.'

'And you haven't heard Hall mention anything about picking up a girl in the van?'

'No. He's one of those quiet types. Probably an axe murderer in his spare time. Still waters, and all that.'

'I'd like you to keep that photo and show it to your other people, see if anybody has seen the girl hanging around the home or anything.'

'I will.'

'Also, can you tell us what sort of worker Brian Hall is?'

'Hall? He works hard enough but he's a bit of a

loner. When people find out he was in borstal when he was a teenager, they naturally think he's a scally. I won't turn my back on him either. Just in case.'

Miller told him the date of the robbery in the jewellery store. 'Would he have been out that day, driving?'

'Hold on, I can check the sheet.' He looked at a chart on the wall. 'Yes. He was out delivering, but as usual, he took ages. God knows what he gets up to.'

Outside, the air was icy cold as the onslaught of snow was well on its way. Miller's teeth were chattering as he got in the car. His phone rang as he started the engine. He listened to the caller before hanging up, and turned to Watt. 'We got a hit on Cindy Stevenson's ex-husband.'

'Let's go and have a word, then. See what he has to say for himself.'

'Another word with him.'

Watt looked puzzled. 'What do you mean?'

Miller told him who they were looking for.

THIRTY-TWO

'Right, lover boy, spit it out,' Stumpy said, coming into Podge's office. They were in their own building, down by Waverley station.

'You know what? You disgust me. You think because we spent all weekend with Vicky I was up to no good?' Despite himself, Podge was grinning.

'Spill the details then, I'm on my way to see Deirdre.' He was leaning on his mail cart.

'Hey, I'm not the sort of guy who goes with a woman and then shouts about it.'

'Listen, I'm going to give you all the details when I've been with Deirdre.'

'I don't want all the filthy details from your escapades.'

'I've nobody else to share them with.'

'Buy a goldfish. That way, it'll be like having family listen to you.'

'You know you want to tell me everything.'

Podge sat back in his chair. 'I really don't.'

'Fuck me.'

'No thanks.'

'I'll just ask Vicky.'

'Don't you dare, Stumpy.'

Stumpy laughed. 'A pint after work. Then you can tell me.'

'You're like body lice; small, and very annoying. Not that I would know...' But Stumpy had already left. Away to push his mail cart.

There was a knock at the door. 'What now? Come to tell me you've got a bigger—'

'Mr Hamilton, we meet again,' Miller said, as he stepped into the room.

'Detective Miller. Have you come to tell me you've arrested Brian Hall?'

Miller walked in, with Watt at his back. 'Not exactly. We'd like to ask you a few questions, back at our station.'

'What? Ask me about what?'

'Do you know Cindy Stevenson?'

Podge could feel his cheeks going red even at the mention of that woman's name. 'No, I don't know who that is.'

Miller looked at Watt before pressing ahead. 'We believe she's your ex-wife.'

'You can believe what you fucking well like,' Podge said, suddenly standing up and pointing a finger at

Miller. Watt was round the desk in a flash, and before he knew what was going on, Podge was bent over the desk and handcuffed.

'What the fuck are you so interested in that bitch for?' Podge screamed.

'Because she was murdered on Saturday night.'

THIRTY-THREE

There she is now, I think to myself, as I drive along in the van. I'm supposed to be at a doctor's appointment, but they won't see me in this thing, a dirty, old white van.

I changed into casual clothes earlier, jeans and an old jacket with a sweatshirt underneath. My uniform, I call it.

The van's lights are all working. I checked everything was okay before leaving. The last thing I need is a cop to pull me over and start getting nosy. The heater is nice and toasty and the young girl will appreciate the warmth, seeing how cold it is outside. I can't believe how gullible some of those young girls are.

I've spent time honing my skills, being nice to them, giving them a bit of chat. Being honest and open. Ha! I'd spoken to this one on the phone before she agreed to come and stay. I had persuaded her that I was an honest, *hard-working man who enjoyed the company of younger women after a bad divorce—*I've never been married—*who was looking for friendship—*I'm actually looking for raging sex—*but you can stay with me in my penthouse. No rent, no bills, no catch! Jesus, I almost believe that last bit.*

'Brilliant,' she'd said, when I had suggested she move out of the shelter. 'I'll be out in a couple of days.'

That had given me a chance to prepare for her.

'Can my friends come up to Edinburgh and visit?' she'd asked.

'Of course they can!' *Can they fuck!*

'My friend Benny would love to come up and stay for a while when I'm settled.'

'That would be fine and dandy!' *It wouldn't be fine, and it most certainly wouldn't be fucking dandy.*

Of course, I've given her an address, somewhere that exists but I'm not connected to. I'd told her it would be frowned upon if the shelter finds out I was letting her stay, that's why I'm meeting her in a café. I told her what bus to get, and to get off in Corstorphine where there was a brilliant little café next to the bank, and I'd meet her there. I was doing business out that way. And she fell for it.

I park the van round the corner in a residential street off St John's Road, the main drag through Corstorphine.

I jump out and walk round to the café, wondering if she got bored and simply left.

But no, she's still there, inside, sitting with a cup of coffee, no doubt wondering if the older man who'd promised her a better life was actually going to show up. At least I haven't groomed her on the internet, pretending to be fifteen.

I wave at the window and she sees me. She pays for the coffee and walks out of the café with her bag.

'Miley!' I say, and smile at her, not sure if she wants a hug or not, so I leave it.

The girl smiles.

'I'm glad you decided to come. It's a lot better than the Washington,' I tell her.

'It's a nice enough place but it will be better being in a proper home. Let me take your bag.'

She hands it over and slips an arm through mine. 'I'm so excited. And nervous.'

'What are you nervous about?'

'All this. Having my stepfather find out I've run away. Knowing my boyfriend will be furious but can't do anything about it.'

My smile is even wider now, and I mean every word I say next. 'You won't ever have to worry about him.'

She turns and smiles at me. 'Thank you.'

'Now, let's get you home and I'll fix you something to eat.' I make sure not to look at the security cameras outside the bank as we walk round the corner to the van.

Miley is the best Christmas present I've ever received.

THIRTY-FOUR

'Look, I haven't seen her in ages. We didn't stay in touch.' Podge sat back in his chair, which was so uncomfortable it was starting to send pins and needles to his feet.

'She died in pain,' Paddy Gibb said. 'A lot of fucking pain.'

'I didn't touch her.'

Miller kept staring at Podge. 'Why don't you tell me a little bit about your relationship with her?'

Podge sighed. 'It was fine at first, but then things went downhill. I started socialising more, and she accused me of having an affair with a woman I was talking to in the pub one night. I wasn't fooling around, but she wasn't convinced. We separated, and she knew she had nothing on me. After two years, we just got divorced, and I handed the cow our house. I just walked away. Bought a new home.'

'You sound bitter, Mr Hamilton,' Miller said.

'It's hard starting over again but I did it.'

'So you hated her,' Miller said.

'I didn't hate her, not enough to kill her anyway. We just drifted apart.'

'You harboured a grudge against her all this time, until you couldn't take it anymore. And on Saturday night, you snapped, and killed her in the cemetery.' Gibb said.

Podge paled. 'What cemetery?'

'You should know, you left her there,' Gibb said.

'I came to tell you about Brian Hall on Friday. Did you arrest him yet?'

'I think you murdered that girl and tried to put us on a false trail,' Gibb said, 'Just so you could create a smokescreen to cover the murder of your ex-wife.'

'So where were you on Saturday night?' Miller said.

'I was with my two friends at our Christmas party. I stayed with them all night and then we just lazed about, just the three of us. My mate and I are staying at our friend's sister's house for a week. House sitting.'

Miller was getting a feeling about this man, and it wasn't one of *I killed my ex-wife and you can't prove it.*

'Warriston,' he said, looking back at Podge. It was a detail they were going to keep to themselves for the time being.

Podge's eyes widened as he looked at Miller.

138

'You're a smart man, detective. You'll go far, but today, you have to go as far as Washington House.'

'Oh, why would that be, sonny?' Gibb said, still not buying what Podge was trying to sell them.

'I was brought up near that cemetery, in Trinity. I still live in the area. My address is in my personnel file. It would be easy enough to access it.'

'So what?' Gibb said.

'Listen, put two and two together, and try not to get five. Miller knows I didn't kill my ex-wife. I can see it in his eyes. Who would want to get my details? Brian Hall. If he knew I was a witness to him being with the murdered girl.'

'You watch your mouth,' Miller said.

'You're saying he went into an office and got on a computer, went through your file and got personal information so he knew about Warriston cemetery?' Gibb made a face and looked at Miller.

'I think you're blowing smoke through your arse,' Gibb said, disliking Podge more with each passing second.

'I told you, I was with two friends all Saturday night.'

'Don't worry, we've got people talking to them too.'

'You're just trying to make me sweat right now until the word comes back. The three of us were at the Christmas do, and then we went back to Vicky's sister's house. It was just the three of us there as the sister is away for a couple of weeks. I haven't even been home since Saturday night. So if it wasn't me, who was it? Oh, I know!'

'Maybe you're all in on it,' Gibb said.

'You don't believe that. What you need to believe is the road Miller's going down. Let me put this little scenario to you.' Podge had been talking fast and now he was thirsty. 'Can I have a drink of water?'

Miller nodded to the uniform who was standing by the door, and the man left.

'Right, listen to this; Brian Hall works for *Home from Home,* spending most of his time at Washington House. It wouldn't be a stretch for him to find information about me. He runs errands and the like. Nobody would give him a second look if he has a badge hanging round his neck saying he's staff. Being maintenance, he has access to every floor. Every office.'

Gibb laughed. Sat back in his chair. 'I think you're telling fairy stories.'

'Just check him out, will you?"

The uniform came back with a glass of water. He had a sheet of paper in his hand as well. 'This is for you, Detective Miller,' he said, putting the plastic cup of water down in front of Podge.

Miller read the words on the paper. It was from Kim; *We traced the phone number that was used by the caller who threatened the woman I went to help on Saturday night. Her name is Vicky and she was with her colleagues Podge and Stumpy (Hamilton and Wilson) all Saturday night, and all day Sunday. The number came from a phone at Washington House.*

Miller passed it over to Gibb, who read it, folded it, and put it on the table. 'So let's just run with your theory for a moment. Tell us what you're thinking.'

'Hall talks to me. He has a thing for my friend, Vicky. He recognised me when the girl bumped the van door into me. Now I'm a witness. He wants me out of the way. So he murders my ex to get back at me. Or to put me behind bars. I've always said he's not as daft as he looks.'

'It still sounds a bit far-fetched,' Gibb said.

'You're detectives. Go and do some detecting. Find out where he was on Saturday night.'

Gibb looked at Miller, indicating for him to suspend the interview. 'Stay put, Hamilton. We'll be back. We need to check something out.' He swept up the paper as he stood, and Miller followed him into the corridor.

They went straight to the investigation suite and into Gibb's office. Paddy sat down in his chair, Miller opposite.

'So he has a cast-iron for all weekend, confirmed so far by his pal, Wilson, who goes by the name *Stumpy*,' Gibb said. 'Jimmy Gilmour interviewed him and now we just need to speak to the female.'

'Right now, we don't have any other suspects, so maybe we should have another look at Brian Hall.'

'And now we're walking the tightrope. You know we can't just go accusing somebody.'

'You're right, but I think we could ask a few more questions, Paddy. We know Hamilton isn't in the frame. Kim's dealing with his friend, Vicky, and the threatening call she got came from the shelter. Let's see where Hall was on Saturday night.'

Gibb drummed his fingers on the desktop and stared at a space on the wall, as if contemplating the demise of his career before making his mind up.

Come on, Paddy, you can do it, Miller thought, mentally willing his boss to make a decision.

Gibb looked at him.

Three, two, one, and you're back in the room, Miller thought.

'Do it. Take Kim to the shelter and have a poke around. Then talk to Hamilton's female friend. See what you can find out on the Hall bloke. If you start to get any hassle, retreat and we'll regroup.'

'We have an excuse for talking to the manager, at least.'

'You just want to know where Hall was on Friday and Saturday. If she gives you any shite, give me a bell, and I'll roast the procurator fiscal.'

Miller knew when Gibb said he'd *roast* Norma Banks, he'd actually be on the phone whining to her. *Begging* might be a better word, but whatever got the job done.

THIRTY-FIVE

Kim pulled the car into the Washington House car park.

'You trust this woman?' Miller said, taking his seatbelt off and getting out of the car into the bitter cold.

'I do. Norma and I worked with Vicky, guiding her through the time when she had to give evidence against her husband.' *Norma, as in her mother, the procurator fiscal.*

They went looking for Vicky after Kim had been told she was working on patient files on the third floor. As they arrived on the third level, Kim saw Vicky along the other end and waved to her. It was late afternoon and it almost seemed as if they were grasping at straws.

'It's been a hell of a day,' Vicky said.

'This is DI Frank Miller, Vicky, the man I was telling you about.'

'Pleased to meet you at last, Frank. I've heard so much about you.'

'Nice to meet you too, Vicky,' he said, as if they were at a social gathering.

'Come on, let's grab a coffee. I'm off the clock in a little while,' she said, leading them along a corridor to the lifts.

'You look knackered, Vicky. Maybe it's a drink you need.'

'I had enough of that at the weekend at our Christmas bash.'

'We hate to ask this, Vicky, but we're interviewing Hamilton. His ex-wife was murdered on Saturday night. Can you tell me if he was with you on Saturday night?'

'Yes, all night. And Sunday too. Oh my God, that's awful. I should call him.'

'Not right now. He's still at the station.'

Kim hit the call button for the lift. The doors slid open and they stepped inside, waiting for the doors to close.

The café was quiet at this time of day, with the cooks preparing the dinner menu, so they ordered coffee and sat at a table.

Vicky took a sip of hers and looked at her friend. This woman wasn't an investigator helping her anymore; Kim had been elevated to "friend" a long time ago. 'I think I've fallen in love again, Kim.'

'Really? That's fantastic. Who is it? Anybody I know.'

'Well... yes, sort of.'

Kim's smile faded. 'It's not Stumpy, is it? I mean, that's okay if it is, of course, but—'

'It's Podge. Ed Hamilton.'

Kim took a sip of her own coffee. 'He seems like a nice guy. How long have you known him?'

'A while now. Oh, I know you think I'm daft, falling for a guy like him, what with all he's been through with his ex-wife, but he's so kind and gentle with me. I've known him for ages, been a friend of his for years, and we just clicked. I love being around him, love everything about him.'

'And he knows about your husband?'

'He does. My divorce will be final in the New Year and then we can see what we want to do with our future.'

'Well, I wish you all the best, Vicky.'

'Thank you. For everything.' Vicky reached a hand over and put it on Kim's. 'I want you to come to my wedding, if Podge and I go the whole distance. Both of you.'

'You know we'll be there.'

I think I'll be the last person Podge would invite to his wedding, Miller wanted to tell her, but bit his tongue.

'I know you still think he might have killed his ex,

but I know he didn't. He was with me, as I said. Besides, he's such a gentleman.'

Vicky smiled and took her hand back. 'When you called me, asking about the files here, I was at my flat. I got a call at work to go home. Somebody turned it over.'

'What?' Kim looked shocked.

'Yes, they threw stuff about, but nothing was taken.'

'Why wasn't I contacted? Your name should have been flagged, so I'd get a notification about anything like this.'

'I don't know. There was a woman there who was the boss of the fingerprint people. They took my prints, so they could differentiate. I told them I get no visitors, so if there are any other prints there, they don't belong to anybody I know. Except you, of course, but they said they had yours on file.'

'You're not staying there, I hope?'

'No. Me, Podge and Stumpy have decided to stay at my sister's house for the time being. Then if things keep happening, and I mean the phone calls and stuff, then we can move to Podge's house. Safety in numbers.'

Miller leaned forward slightly. 'Do you trust those two guys, Vicky?'

'I do, Frank. They're the first men I've ever known who've treated me well.'

'I want you to stay at your own office in Market Street. I don't want you coming here again,' Kim said.

Vicky looked concerned. 'Why? What's wrong?'

'Don't panic because I'm here with you, but whoever made the call to you on Saturday night, made it from here. I just found out whose office it came from.'

'Who is it?' Vicky asked.

THIRTY-SIX

'From here?' Heather Dougal said. 'From my office?'

'Yes,' Miller said, stepping farther into the room. 'Somebody called from here on Saturday night.'

'I don't see how that's possible.'

'Somebody found it easy enough. I had the intelligence unit check it out. They definitely used your phone to make a call.' Kim had asked Vicky to stay in the filing area, where she was authorised to be working anyway.

'Well, I can assure you it wasn't me. I was at home on Saturday night. I was alone but I was watching TV.'

'Nobody's accusing you, Miss Dougal. It was a man who called from here, so I need to know who has access.'

Heather visibly relaxed. 'Unfortunately, this is sometimes like Waverley Station, with a lot of people coming-and-going. This door is locked, but anybody with half a mind and a plastic card could open it.'

'Are residents allowed in here?' Kim asked.

'No, just staff.'

'Like Brian Hall,' Miller said, matter-of-factly. 'Does he work weekends?'

Heather looked unsure for a moment before answering. 'Yes, Brian works some weekend shifts.'

Kim said. 'Can he come and go here as he pleases?'

'Yes. All the maintenance crew can. This is a huge building as you can see, and it takes a lot of staff to run it, so there are staff here all the time.'

'So it's possible for a maintenance guy to come in here on Saturday night, be walking about and nobody would question him?'

'Yes. They're here all the time, twenty-four seven.'

'And of course, they have keys for everywhere?' Miller said. 'Including your office?'

'Yes.'

'Could you get me his personal details, Heather?'

'I'm sorry, I can't. Unless you came here with a warrant to arrest him, then there's the privacy law. I personally can't hand out that information.' She looked at them apologetically. 'You don't have a warrant, do you?'

'No,' Miller said.

'Thanks. We'll be in touch if we need any more information,' Kim said, knowing the woman was right.

They went back along to the corridor that led

down to the administration suite. Found Vicky standing talking to another woman. She smiled when she saw Kim and excused herself.

'I hate to admit it, but I was hiding in the filing room until somebody came in, then I was speaking to my friend there, just so I felt safe.'

'Good idea.'

'While I was in the filing room, I had a look around.' They'd reached the lift and when they were the only three in it, Vicky carried on. 'Podge's file had been taken out and put back in a different spot. Just a few names away, but it was out of alphabetical order. As if somebody had taken it out and thought they were putting it back in the same spot, but hadn't, without realising it.'

'Don't say anymore just now.' They walked out of the building, into the rush hour darkness. 'Did you drive here?'

'I usually do, but I got the bus down. With the three of us living at my sister's house, my car is at my own flat. Podge drives us all into work.'

'We're going to drive you home. Don't come back here, Vicky. I'm going to have my boss make a phone call to your work and tell them you're in danger.'

'Okay.'

They got to Kim's car. Frank said he would sit in the back. It gave him time to think. If Brian Hall decided he would have a go with the wee polis lassie, they'd all be arguing over who got to switch off his life support machine.

'I did something else, Kim, something I could be fired for.'

Kim smiled in the darkness of the car. 'I'm listening.'

'I looked at Brian Hall's file.' She looked over at the detective and felt a shiver run down her spine. 'I know why he was put into the secure unit when he was a boy.'

THIRTY-SEVEN

'So, what do you think of the place?' I ask, rubbing my hair with a towel as I come into the living room. I've put on a bathrobe and pad about in bare feet. I walk over to the drinks cabinet and pour myself a brandy. 'Want one?'

'Yes, thanks.'

'So, to answer my question, what do you think?'

'I like it. You have a beautiful place.'

'Thank you. I bought it before the banks screwed us all over.' This is a lie obviously; I don't own the place but if it impresses her and gets her into my bed quicker, what the hell?

I walk over with both glasses after throwing my towel onto the back of a dining chair. 'You can stay as long as you like,' I tell her, but in reality, she can stay as long as she's satisfying me.

Miley takes a glass and we clink before taking a sip.

Cheers, Cheryl. I laugh inside at her pseudonym, Miley. Good Lord.

Cheryl Atkinson is her name. Age seventeen from South London. I made sure I poked around beforehand. What youngsters fail to realise, once your shit is up on social media, it doesn't go away.

'Cheers. I'm so glad you let me come here.'

'I'm glad you're here.' I'm confident that she won't be able to resist my charms after she sees the expensive watch on my wrist. If she finds that she can resist me, then she'll be out the door, simple as that. I've had to show the door to a few of them in the past.

She puts the glass down on a side table and stands up. Walks over and kisses me.

'I've always loved older men. I've been with a couple and you always look after a young girl like me. When I heard your voice on the phone, I realised you're the first old man I've fallen in love with.'

I feel my heart explode. Fucking old man? Even that other dumb bitch from Birmingham managed to call me "experienced", not old. I know she isn't going to last long here. Maybe I'll boot her back out between Christmas and New Year. That'll teach her a lesson.

First, though, I want to have her and enjoy feeling her nakedness beneath me.

I walk her through to the bedroom where she unties my robe.

Ten minutes later, I'm finished and sweating again, so I have another quick shower.

'Where are you going?' Miley asks, sitting up in bed, using the sheets to cover her breasts.

'Don't wait up. I have to meet clients.' The lie rolls off my tongue easily.

'Okay, honey, I'll be here.'

I go through to the walk-in dressing room. I feel as if I'm in Hollywood when I go into the room. I can admire my expensive clothes and watches, without being interrupted.

Ten minutes later, I'm pulling my Porsche 911 in front of the house. I may as well enjoy it before it's repossessed. Jesus Christ, my whole body feels like it's a piece of razor wire. Gina opens the door and smiles at me. 'Come in for a minute while I get my coat.'

I step over the threshold and close the door roughly behind me.

Gina whirls round, shocked for a second.

'I want you, Gina. I want you right now. I couldn't love you more if I tried.'

Her eyes widen at the 'L' word and she wraps her arms around me as I kiss her hard.

'Let's go, lover boy,' she says, pulling away from me. 'Dinner can wait. I've got a starter that you don't want to miss.'

She takes me through to the bedroom.

THIRTY-EIGHT

'Just try and relax, Kim,' Miller said. 'You don't need the weight of the world on your shoulders.'

'Vicky's worried Hall is going to come after her, Frank. I wouldn't be able to forgive myself if something happened to her.'

They were both wrapped up warmly and holding hands as they walked through the European Market in Princes Street Gardens, screams coming from the rides.

'At least she has those two guys looking after her.'

'How did Gibb feel about letting Hamilton go?'

'He was on board with it. Even though he didn't like Hamilton's attitude, there was no arguing with his alibi, especially since the woman who gave him it was a friend of yours.'

'She's a friend now because of what I was helping her through.'

'You know what Gibb's like.'

Emma was holding onto Miller's other hand and he liked the feel of her little gloved hand in his.

'Frank, I can't wait to be a big girl so I can go on the flying chairs. That looks fun!' She looked up at him. 'Do you think Santa will go on them after he leaves the presents?'

'I think he has enough fun riding about with his reindeer. He doesn't need the swings. But we should let your mum go on them and we can stay down here and watch her scream.'

'Can we?' she said, jumping up and down.

'Emma, Frank's kidding.' Kim smiled at her daughter and patted her head.

'Next time,' Miller whispered to the little girl.

'I wanted to put a tail on Hall, but the PF isn't having any of it. She feels any competent defence lawyer would be able to throw anything we gathered from it out of court. That sort of crap. If there's anything against Hall, it has to stick and so far, we have a sighting from a sketchy witness.'

'It's frustrating, Kim, but that's the game we're in. Sometimes the bad get more protection than the good.'

'I know you're right.' She stopped and looked at the multi-coloured Ferris wheel, as it turned round and round, filled with anonymous faces enjoying the thrill.

'You heard what Vicky said, Frank; Hall tried to rape a neighbour's daughter, so they had a specialist look at him. They deemed him a menace to society and put him in a young offenders institution. They let him out under minimal care because they think he has a low IQ, but don't think he's a danger.'

'We'd have to know more of his background. Like, how long was he in there, and what the official reports said.'

'I'd put money on, *he couldn't stop himself.*'

They walked past the vendors, their stalls well lit, an icy air blowing through the gardens.

'Why don't we go home and have hot chocolate?' Miller said.

'I'd like that, Frank,' Emma said, squeezing his hand harder.

Miller knew that the love he felt for this little girl was genuine and as each day passed, he thought of her more and more as his own daughter.

They walked down the Waverley Bridge then up Cockburn Street. Back in the flat, they chatted about Christmas coming up as Miller put the kettle on.

'This will be your first Christmas dinner at my folks,' Kim said. 'You nervous?'

'Well, your mother is Norma Banks, the procurator fiscal, so what's there to be nervous about?'

She laughed. 'You'll have my dad on your side.'

'We'll both be sleeping off the tryptophan after dinner. It's what us men do.'

'So we get landed with washing the dishes? Think again, Miller.' She smiled and kissed him.

They made the hot chocolate and sat at the dining table, while Emma had hers in the living room where

Charlie, their cat, was sleeping. They heard her asking the cat if he wanted to play dolls.

Then Kim said something that had been building up inside. 'I know it's only been a few years since you lost Carol, and she was a fantastic wife, and I'm here now, and—'

He leaned over and kissed her. 'Natural progression. I love you, don't forget that.' Harvey Levitt, the force psychiatrist, would have been proud of him.

'I love you too, Frank Miller.'

They made small talk for a few minutes before more shoptalk.

'Where does Brian Hall live?' Miller asked, after taking a sip of his hot chocolate.

'I don't know to be honest.'

'I can't get out of my head what Hamilton was saying about Hall being seen with the dead girl before she was found.'

'Vicky seems to think that Hall acts as if he's a daft laddie, but he isn't as daft as he looks, is he?'

'No.'

THIRTY-NINE

The investigation had slowed down by the middle of the week. Percy Purcell was back from Aberdeen and Miller had filled him in on the murder in the cemetery.

'How were things up in Aberdeen?'

'I never knew how much crap I owned until I started to box it all up. Most of it was in storage but we got it down. I'm knackered though. I needed to come back for a rest.'

'When will Suzie be here?'

'Not until after Christmas. She's spending it with her folks.'

'Kim and I are looking forward to seeing her again. We'll have you both round for dinner. Jack and Samantha are in New York, so it would be the four of us.'

'What about wee Emma?'

'I'm sure Granny Norma will be delighted to have her round for a night.'

Now, Miller was back in his office and took a call from the manager of the *Home from Home* warehouse, Len McLennan, who confirmed Hall had turned up for a shift that morning to help run supplies to the shelter in the Grange.

'Who has access to the van keys?' Miller asked.

'Just me, and I give them to the driver.'

'Are they left there in your office at the warehouse?'

'Are you kidding me? If I left them here, that hoor would be back at the weekend doing a removal with it. No, they're locked away. I give them to him at the start of his shift and he gives me them back when he's done for the day. Nice guy, but I'd trust him as far as I could spit.'

Miller thanked him before he hung up and then he called Kim, told her what he wanted, and she phoned back five minutes later.

'My boyfriend is a genius,' she said to him

'I know. Keep feeding my ego.'

'You wondered if Hall might own a white van. He doesn't. Somebody we know does though.'

'Ed Hamilton?'

'No, his friend, Mickey Wilson. Stumpy, as he calls him.'

Miller looked out his office window. Snow covered the roofs of the tenements behind their building. He'd often wondered what it would have been like to have lived here hundreds of years ago, when people threw their garbage out the windows to the streets below.

'So let's assume Hamilton *is* correct, and he *did* see Hall with the dead girl?'

'Do you suppose they were working together? Hall and the girl?'

'Let me make a call.' He dialled a number, spoke to somebody, and waited for a reply before hanging up. 'She went missing three months ago. What if he met her, befriended her, and got her trust?'

Kim sat down. 'What if he encouraged her to do that robbery? If that was something he was building up to? What if they started small and built up to armed robbery?'

'Okay, let's say he did groom her; where was she living?'

Kim let out a deep breath. 'Not at the shelter.'

'So where would he have taken her?'

Kim looked at him. 'Home.'

FORTY

'Coming out on the lash tonight, Podgy boy?' Stumpy was pushing the mail cart around the admin area of the hospital and had stopped by Podge's office.

'I know we go out at the end of the week, Stumps, but don't you think we should stay in with Vicky? It *is* Christmas Eve after all.'

'Dearie me, if I didn't know you better, I'd say you were after something from her.'

'Listen, Stumpy,' Podge looked around to make sure nobody was listening, 'We're trying to keep this quiet since her divorce hasn't been finalised yet.'

'And because her husband's a nutter.'

'I already told you he fights like a fanny.'

'But he might not sign the papers if he knows you're throwing Vicky a length.'

'Jesus, what kind of talk is that?'

Stumpy laughed. 'I thought we could maybe make a foursome tonight.'

'I do hope you mean four of us go out for a drink!'

'Of course I do. If that's what you want it to mean.' He grinned.

'You should be so lucky.' Podge sat back in his chair. 'I'm guessing Dirty Deirdre from Dalkeith is meeting you tonight.'

'Yes, she is. I thought we could all have a drink and then go clubbing. I can shake my thing on the dance floor again.'

'Please, God, tell me he means his little baseball bat.'

'I meant my groove, Podgy boy, my groove. You know when I get going, I can't stop.'

'I know when you start talking pish, you can't stop.'

'So I'll tell my girlfriend we'll meet at seven?'

'Girlfriend, now? Don't you tie them up with duct tape before you call them *girlfriend*?'

'I've got something that bypasses the need for duct tape.'

'Oh, I forgot; your little baseball bat.'

'Something a lot better than that.'

'I'm not going to ask. I don't want to be put off my turkey dinner.' He leant back in his office chair. 'Stumpy, you go ahead. I'd just feel safer if I stayed at home with Vicky.'

'Yeah, yeah, you dress it up any way you want to, Podge. Besides, it'll be four of us. It'll be a laugh.'

Podge sighed. 'Go on then. I'm sure Vicky will be up for a night out.'

'Good man.'

'I assume you'll be home for dinner before you go out?'

'Yes, dad. I'm not springing for a scran for her on the first date. I want to see how she acts first. Maybe next time.'

'Right, Romeo, sod off, I've work to do. I'll tell Vicky I'm cooking tonight. Or we'll order Chinese, one of the two.'

'Chinese. I've tasted your cooking before. I don't want to be shitting through the eye of a needle when I'm out tonight.'

'Yeah, as romantic evenings go, that wouldn't make a good first impression.'

'Catch you later, buddy.'

Podge shook his head and smiled as his friend wheeled the mail cart out. Nobody ever questioned Stumpy as he walked round the floors with the mail. Hiding in plain sight, he called it.

He picked up his phone and called Vicky, feeling, for the first time in a week, he could relax a bit. There'd been no sign of Hall. The police had tagged him a few times, and he was doing nothing out of the ordinary. *Maybe I was wrong about him. Maybe Hall is as harmless as the next man.*

And it was this sort of thinking that got people killed.

FORTY-ONE

Miller was working at his desk when he got a call from the front desk downstairs.

'It's in connection with the Sabrina Hailes' murder. It's a family member. A young man.'

'Okay, send him up.'

Miller looked at Sabrina's photo on the whiteboard, wondering how he was going to explain to this relative that the young girl had been found dead on a cold, wet beach.

'Kim?'

She looked up from her desk as Miller walked into her office. 'What's up, Frank?'

'The desk sergeant's sending somebody up. A member of Sabrina Hailes' family. Can you come with me? I want to speak to him in the conference room.'

'Sure.' She got up and followed him out. 'I thought nobody was coming up to identify her?'

'That's what they said.'

They waited in the corridor and a few minutes later, a uniform brought a young man up.

'I'm Dave Hailes. Sabrina was my sister.'

Kim looked at him with compassion. After the family had told them nobody would be coming to Edinburgh to identify the girl, this was the last person she'd expected to see.

'Mr Hailes. Please, come in here.' They entered the conference room, the uniform following. There was a large rectangular table surrounded by chairs, and a window looked out onto High Street below. 'Would you like a coffee?'

'That would be great. Black. I just drove up here and I'm beat.' His Birmingham accent was thick.

'Could you get Mr Hailes a coffee, please?' Miller asked the uniform, who nodded and left the room.

Hailes looked haggard, as if he hadn't slept for a week.

'I'm sorry for your loss, Mr Hailes,' Kim said.

The uniform came back from the vending machine and silently handed the coffee over.

'Thanks.' He nodded as he drank his coffee. 'I'm sorry it took so long for one of us to get up here, but my parents aren't interested. Sabrina was always getting into trouble. Always messing about with boys.'

'Had she run away before?'

'No. She'd been picked up by the police and brought home after getting into trouble, but she was always fighting. My parents practically disowned her when she was expelled from school. They couldn't control her. Me and my brother are in our twenties, but she was a late baby and my parents are too old to deal with her.'

'Do you know why she'd get it in her head to run away now?' Miller asked.

Hailes drank more coffee. 'My dad used to beat her with a belt. She would fight back, but she was getting fed up with it. She said there had to be more to life. Next thing we knew, she was gone.'

'And your parents didn't bother about that?' Miller said.

'No. They were glad to get rid of her.' He looked between them both. 'I know what you're thinking; why didn't he try and stop his father from beating his sister? I tried. I really did, but he would get into me too.'

'Nobody's blaming you, pal,' Miller said. 'We're just here to catch her killer.'

'Had Sabrina contacted you since she came up here?' Kim asked.

'One time. She called me and said she was fine, she'd met an older bloke, and he was fantastic. He was going to look after her. The place she was staying in was fantastic. She said she would call again, but she didn't.'

'Did she tell you his name?'

'No.'

'What about a street address?'

'No, but she did say that it was in an expensive area.' He looked at them both. 'They all say that though, don't they? Those perverts who touch kids. They pretend they're something they're not, and then the kid goes missing. I'll bet that's who she hooked up with. A perv.'

Suddenly, Hailes broke down. Kim got up and put an arm around his shoulders until the crying subsided.

'I'm sorry about that,' he said, sniffing and taking a hanky out of his pocket.

'Oh God, don't be sorry.' She sat back down. 'Do you think you'll be up to identifying your sister?'

He took a deep breath and let it out, composing himself. 'That's why I'm here. If my parents won't come up, then I'm not going to let Sabrina pass without a family member identifying her.'

'I'll have an officer take you down to the mortuary. Thank you for coming. Do you have somewhere to stay while you're here?'

'Yes, I got a room in a small bed and breakfast. I'm driving back tomorrow. Although it's hardly going to be a merry Christmas.'

Kim was wondering if maybe Sabrina had got involved with a man who'd groomed her to help rob a jewellery store, and then when she was surplus to requirements, he'd killed her. The question was could he be doing it again? And had he done it in the past?

Miller got DS Jimmy Gilmour and one of the

detective constables to take Dave Hailes to the mortuary.

Just as Kim sat back down in the incident room, her phone rang.

'It's Maggie Parks, Kim.' She was the head of the Identification Branch.

'Hi, Maggie. What's up?'

'Sorry it's taken so long, but everything's backed up. We got a result from the fingerprint sweep we did in your friend Vicky's house. The lab just got back to me. They ran the prints through the system, and apart from you and her, there was one unknown print. But we got a match from the cistern handle. It belongs to a man called Ed Hamilton.'

FORTY-TWO

That's the beauty of the little spy cameras; they can be anywhere, hidden in a clock, or a light bulb or a picture frame. Almost anything. The ones I'd put in the flat had audio so I could hear as well as see.

I make it a habit to check in every so often. Not paranoia, but when you're playing my game, you have to keep on your toes.

So when I look in that afternoon and see what's going on, I move fast.

As I enter my flat, I close the front door behind me. It doesn't matter if the stranger hears me or not. I know where he is. I've checked my phone before coming in and make enough noise at the door so he'll hide. Fore-warned is forearmed, my stepfather used to teach me when I was little.

I walk through to the living room. The girl is standing there, drinking and dancing to music playing on the radio. She stops when she sees me. Laughs and turns the music off.

'I was wondering when you would turn up.' She drinks more red wine, letting some of it slurp over her lips onto the beige carpet. 'Oops.'

I look at her wrist, knowing I can't be too long. The man in the other room won't take his time coming through and that will only make things harder for me.

'Give me the watch,' I say to her. The little Cockney bitch. She's wearing the Calibre de Cartier, with the black rubber strap and eighteen carat rose gold case. It's too big for her wrist, but she flaunts it in front of my face. Laughs.

'Do you like what I found?'

'Nice choice. Now give it back to me.'

'You know I can't do that. It'll go down a treat at my local. I should get a few hundred quid for this.'

'Just give it to me and I won't hurt you.' Not quite true, but if it helps her relax until I kill her, I'll tell her anything.

She laughs at my words, not taking them seriously. I'm going to enjoy killing this little fucker.

'Don't I deserve it? After all, I'm your little whore now. Or did you think I'd fallen for your game? Get me in here, have me whenever you like and then dump me when you get bored? I deserve a little bonus, don't you think?'

'Last time. Give it to me, and then get your stuff together. You're leaving.'

'You want it, you fucking take it.' Her eyes move towards the living room door. I look in the mirror above the fireplace and see there's nothing there. Yet. He's in the bedroom, hiding.

'Now, now, where are your manners?' I say to her. I don't move closer. That would only make her do something drastic. Right now, there's a comfortable space between us, a space that she thinks is keeping her safe.

She's stalling for time and it might have worked on somebody less evil than me, but I trust nobody.

She grins and slops more wine into her mouth. 'I was having a little look-see round here and guess what else I found?' Her London accent is as if she's just stepped off the set of a soap opera.

I sit down on the couch. 'Come on, sit down, and you can tell me what you found.'

'Nah, I'm alright. I'll just stand here.' She flashes the watch around. 'We found a few of these. And we're keeping them, you do know that, right?'

She doesn't realise she said "We" and had I not already known he was there, that would have given her game away.

She's still trying to distract me, and I've no doubt, if I remain seated, then I will die. But I have only one reason for sitting down; before I stand back up, my hand slips down the side of the settee and brings out the hammer I'd put there earlier. It's a ball-peen hammer, with a normal hammer head on one end and a ball on the other. I'd selected it at a DIY store, something that

172

wasn't too big and clumsy but had enough weight to do the job.

The forehead will bleed if you cut it, but won't if it's struck hard. Ever bumped your head into something and ended up with a huge bump and bruise but no cut? This is what a hammer does.

It's not an exact science. You have a couple of seconds before they register what's happening. I bring the hammer up, keeping it close to my body. If I bring it up and swing it right back before trying to hit her, she'll have time to defend herself. So I keep it close to my side, bring it up to my shoulder and bring it forward, hard and fast.

I aim for the part of the face just above the nose so the hammer will break the nose bone, hopefully driving it into the brain, killing her instantly.

This girl is young and has quick reflexes, but ultimately not quick enough. She does move slightly though, as her eyes take in the sight before her, me standing up, bringing the hammer up, and swinging it towards her face.

She moves. By that time though, the hammer is on its way forward with my weight behind it, gaining momentum with each split-second.

The hammerhead catches her square on the forehead, enough to leave an impression of the tool. She lets out a confused uugghh noise, as if she can't decide whether to scream or shout. The impact from the hammer will cause her brain to move to the back of the *skull, just enough to shock her. As her coherence is compromised, I step in closer, still slightly to her right to get a good swing at her, and bring the hammer in again.*

This time, there's no noise. She falls backwards, still alive but her brain dealing with the trauma. The glass of wine flies from her hand, splashing the carpet. I don't want her dead yet. It will mean I will have to clean up the mess her body leaves behind. The wine can be cleaned later.

FORTY-THREE

I watch the girl breathing, but only just. Her body muscles will relax when she dies, and I'll deal with her before that happens, but right now, I have more to worry about.

Like the man who's coming into the living room behind me.

'Cheryl! What the fuck have you done to her?' He looks between her and me.

His voice is rising, so I'll have to take care of him quickly.

He stops as his mind registers what's happened to his girlfriend. 'I'll fucking kill you!' he says.

Again, timing is everything. I step in to meet the imminent attack. Pivot on my left foot and strike out with my right, catching the inside of his right knee as he's facing me. I duck when I pivot as I see his arm pulled back as he prepares for a roundhouse punch. His knee cracks as it dislocates, his leg bending at an angle that nature hadn't intended it to.

I straighten up and kick him between the legs as he's going down, starting to scream in pain. I have to shut him up quickly. The adrenaline pushes me forward and I stamp down on his throat, my boot heel flattening his Adam's apple. His screaming stops, to be replaced by a wheezing, gurgling sound as one hand goes to his throat and the other starts beating the carpet. I step back and kick him hard under the chin.

He's still alive as I go through to the bedroom. I'd put a sheet of heavy gauge plastic up in the attic and brought it down earlier. Just folded and tucked away in the back of the wardrobe with the plastic bags and cable ties, so even if they were found, nobody would give it a second thought.

He's still incapacitated. I take the thick plastic bag and slip it over his head, followed by the large cable tie. I pull the plastic tie tight round his neck, almost shutting off his air supply, but he doesn't have much longer anyway. The blood from his ruptured throat will kill him.

I then wrap him in the plastic sheet. Drag him through the bedroom and into the dressing room. He can stay here for a little while. Then I'll dump him. I take the other sheet and put Cheryl on it, then lift her head up before twisting it hard. Something snaps and the light goes out in her eyes.

After she's dead, I wrap her in the polythene. Then I drag her through to the bedroom to join her boyfriend.

I have a large trunk in the dressing room that I keep sweaters in that I wear in the winter. When I was at the DIY store buying the hammer, I bought four casters and screwed them onto the bottom of the trunk. It looks fashionable, like some people will try and take a piece of old driftwood and make treasure out of it. I empty it out and wheel it into the bedroom and get the boyfriend in first, bending him before rigor sets in.

I do two trips down to the van, taking the elevator, preparing a story of how I'm having a clear out. I really was taking the trash out! However, I meet nobody, and before I know it, they're both in the back of the van.

There are no security cameras down in the garage, which is a stupid oversight. But it makes things less complicated for me.

Back up to the apartment with the trunk and I have one final look through to see if there's anything I've missed, but there's nothing obvious.

FORTY-FOUR

Vicky knew Kim had told her not to come back to Washington House on her own again, but she was finishing a case for a homeless man who was waiting to be transferred here. With it being Christmas Eve, half the staff were still out on their extended lunch and the day was getting away from them.

Podge had called her, and it felt good to hear his voice again. He told her Stumpy had suggested they go on a foursome; meet the new woman in his life. Deirdre from accounts. She didn't know the woman, but maybe she'd turn out to be okay. She liked Stumpy a lot so it might be fun.

She told Podge she probably wouldn't be finished at the same time they were, but since she was at the Washington, she'd just meet them in town. They could all go out for Chinese after Christmas. It would be nice to go out and not look at her watch every five minutes, knowing somebody was waiting at home to slap her about, as she'd been when she was married.

She walked along the admin corridor and went into the file room. She'd get this done and get off.

Mission accomplished, she decided to pull Brian Hall's personnel file once more, and scan through it. Even though she knew it was an offence that would get her fired, if she was caught, she needed to know about the strange man her boyfriend – yes, that's right, her *boyfriend!* not just her *friend* anymore! – had befriended.

She took off her jacket and sat down at a table that had been put there for the very purpose of sitting and reading, and flipped open the file again. The updated photo of the man looked back at her. Vicky's breath caught in her throat, and she thought she was going to explode, until she let her breath out again.

Brian Hall had been put away in Wardrop House at age fifteen, for touching young girls, and had been caught attempting to rape a neighbour's daughter.

Now she started reading more of his case notes.

He'd stayed there until he was twenty-one.

She thought back to the weekend when she'd felt she was really getting to know Podge, as they'd opened up to each other about their lives. They'd sat and talked for hours, and until that moment, she hadn't believed in the nonsense of finding your soulmate, but as she let Podge make love to her, she knew she'd truly found hers.

He'd told her how he'd had a tough marriage. He'd only just recently found out he had a sister. One he had connected to, and they were just getting to know each other.

And this man Brian Hall had been trying to get to know her better. He was nothing but a pervert.

She quickly closed the file and shrugged her jacket back on. Put the file away, probably in the wrong place, but she didn't care. Nothing mattered now. She sent Podge a quick text, wanting to be far away from this horrible place.

She rushed downstairs and out into the dark car park, pulling her phone from her pocket. Dialled Kim's number. It went to voicemail. Snow was falling again, starting to cover the roads, making it slippery under foot.

Then she saw Stumpy's van. The headlights flashed and it pulled forward, the full beams blinding her. Podge must have come to pick her up. She felt a wave of relief flood through her as the van pulled up. She opened the door and climbed in, and heard the peep from the phone for her to leave a message.

'I found out something about Brian Hall—' she started to say, as she looked over at Podge. But it wasn't Podge.

FORTY-FIVE

'Relax, she'll be there,' Stumpy said, as he spoke to Podge on his mobile phone.

'I can't get hold of her now, Stumpy. She sent me that text over an hour ago.'

'What did it say again?'

I found out something about Hall. We need to talk. I'm calling Kim Smith.

'Who's Kim Smith?'

'Fuck's sake, Stumps, try and keep on board. She's that investigator who grilled you and Vicky the other day.'

'Oh, her. She was nice. I think she wanted a ride on the *Stumpycoaster*.'

'Will you concentrate for one minute? If your mind's not on your dinky, it's getting pished. I need you to stay focused. I'm going to make another call so I'll phone you back.'

'I'll be here. I'm waiting for Deirdre but she's running late.'

Podge hung up.

The bar was starting to fill up and Podge was glad to be outside in the fresh air. He was worried about Vicky. Running late was one thing, but not answering her phone was something else. When he couldn't get through to her again, he called the station and asked to be put through to Kim Smith.

'Doctor Smith? This is Ed Hamilton.'

'What can I do for you, Mr Hamilton?' Neutral tone, expecting a tirade of abuse or something.

'It's Vicky. I can't get hold of her. Have you heard from her at all?'

'I haven't. I've been busy dealing with something. Hold on while I check my mobile.' She kept him on hold while she checked her phone, 'Nothing. When was the last time you saw her?'

'Today at work. She had to go to Washington House to deal with a resident's transition. Me and Stumpy were going to have a night out with her, but she hasn't turned up.'

'Where are you right now, Mr Hamilton?'

'I'm in the bar of the LearmonthHotel, just round the corner from where we're staying at Vicky's sister's house.'

'I'm going to the Washington now.'

'I'll meet you there.'

'No, you won't. This is police business.'
'Try and stop me.'
Podge hung up.

FORTY-SIX

Kim Smith was just coming out of the entrance to the shelter when Podge arrived. He'd caught a taxi right away. He walked past a few uniforms. 'Any sign of her?' he asked.

She shook her head. 'No. One of the officers found this in the car park.' She held up the iPhone.

'Can I see it?'

Kim looked dubious but handed him the phone.

'If it's hers, there should be selfies on there she took at last Saturday's night out.' He scrolled through and quickly found the selfies he'd mentioned. 'It's her phone. Hall took her. There's no way she'd call me and then suddenly leave her phone in the car park.'

'Maybe she dropped it.'

'You don't believe that any more than I do. Was the call disconnected when you found it?'

'Yes.'

'So somebody ended the call and threw it away. And we all know who that was.'

Miller came out of the doors, looking for Kim. 'I found something on the security tapes you should see.'

'I'm going back in. You stay here.'

'Okay.'

She followed Miller inside and along to the security office.

Podge took the opportunity to pocket Vicky's phone before Kim remembered he was the one holding it.

'I found this,' Miller said. 'There's Vicky walking about inside, and then she leaves, but watch this.'

The security officer moved the frames of the images and they saw Vicky talking on her phone in the car park. Then a white van pulled up and she got inside. The headlights were on full and they couldn't see the driver. They could clearly see him throw Vicky's phone out the window before he drove off. There was no number plate on the back of the van.

'Why would she just get in the van with him?' Kim asked.

'She thought it was me,' Podge said, opening the door fully.

'I told you to stay outside.'

Podge ignored her. 'I've been driving my friend's van. Maybe she thought I was there to pick her up. It's the same type of van.'

Kim looked at the time stamp. 'So she was taken in

a van similar to the one you've been driving, and then you're suddenly here. If you have an alibi for that time, you'd better cough it up right now.'

'Oh for Christ's sake. I was in the bar of that hotel, like I told you. Call them and find out, but do it fast. Vicky's in danger.'

Kim went into the corridor and came back a few minutes later. 'Okay, so you're in the clear.'

'You need to send somebody round to Hall's house.'

Miller looked at Kim. 'Can you call the PF and ask her to get a warrant?'

'I will. I'll have her email it to me. She won't have a problem doing it. She knows all the judges so one of them will accommodate her.'

Podge ran a hand over his short hair. 'Jesus, he could be anywhere with her, doing anything to her.'

'We don't know for an absolute fact it's him,' Kim said, going for a soothing voice, and not quite managing it. The phone on the other end started ringing so she excused herself.

'She was here, we know Hall works here so he walks about unnoticed, and now she got in a van. He sometimes drives a van for the shelter. Unless there's another random psycho out there, I'd put my money on it being Hall,' Podge said.

'I'm starting to think you're right,' Miller said.

FORTY-SEVEN

Podge left the shelter and walked over to the Argyle on Argyle Place, round the corner. It was a small pub, friendly atmosphere. It was starting to get busy, and he thought it would be a nice place to bring Vicky some time, if the police found her safe.

He bought a pint, found a quiet corner and called his friend but hung up. He wanted to be with his thoughts just now. God, what was happening to him? He'd been with women in the past of course, but he hadn't felt anything like he felt for Vicky.

The pain of Hall taking her was like a spear ramming through his gut. Kim Smith had found something out but she hadn't shared with him. Even though it was *his* girlfriend who'd been taken.

He didn't know what to do. All he could think about was Vicky and what Hall was probably doing to her right now. He took her phone out of his pocket. Opened up the photos.

She had told him she loved him, and now he knew that Hall wanted her for himself, and one sure way was to get him, Hamilton, out of the way.

And now she was going to die because of him.

Well, not if I can help it, sweetheart. He got up from his table and went outside, making a call to Kim Smith.

'Jesus, your timing's perfect,' she said.

'Listen, I have to know if you know where Vicky is.'

'Like I told you before, this is police business.'

'Kim, listen to me; Vicky's your friend, and now my girlfriend. If you don't have a clue where she is, I might know.'

There was a moment's silence on the other end.

'There's no sign of them.' She knew she was throwing him a bone, but she really liked Vicky and would hate for anything to happen to her.

'I think I know where he might be.'

He told her where, and the rest of the information and went outside, unable to sit still.

After he hung up, he called Stumpy. 'How much you had to drink, wee man?'

'Well, not so much that I couldn't run a hundred yards to a river if my arse was on fire.'

'Is your girlfriend there yet?'

'No.'

'Bump her, Stumpy. You need to come and get me. How long will it take?'

'Ten seconds.'

'What?'

'I'm looking at you. I only just parked up. Deirdre called and said she'd meet us later, so I figured I'd bring the van up here. This is the closest pub to the hospital, so I was going to wait inside for you.'

Podge looked over and, for once, couldn't have been happier to see his friend.

He walked over to Stumpy and stood looking at him as his friend rolled the window down. 'I need to borrow the van, Stumps. I can't take you with me. I think I know where Hall's taken Vicky. It's too dangerous.'

Stumpy grinned. 'Listen, if you think I'm going to pass up the chance to give Brian Hall a good belting, you're even dafter than you look. I'm coming with you.'

Podge smiled. 'I think another angel just got its wings.'

FORTY-EIGHT

Miller stood holding a cup of coffee. It was tasteless, brown water, but he drank it nonetheless.

'I'm having my doubts about this guy Hamilton. Something's not quite right.' He was standing looking at the security monitors.

'What do you mean? Kim asked.

'He's telling us things, and we even let him in here for God's sake, but there's just something jarring with me.'

'He seemed eager to help us.'

'*Too* eager maybe.'

'You think this is all smoke and mirrors with him?'

'Could be.' He sipped the lukewarm liquid before putting the cup down. 'Didn't you tell me he was picking up your friend in his van to take her to their work's dance the other night?'

'I did.'

Miller asked the security guard to roll the tape back to where they could see Vicky walking out towards the van. They still couldn't see the licence plate or the driver, but Miller got him to freeze the frame anyway. Then he looked at Kim again.

'Obviously, Hamilton was in here with us, and you called the bar so we know he was there. But what about his friend?'

'The one he calls Stumpy? Mickey Wilson?' Kim looked sceptical.

'Yeah, him.'

'He doesn't look the sort, Frank. He's a small man. I can't see him doing this.'

'You know, when you're a big guy and a fight breaks out in the pub, it's the little guy you've got to watch out for.'

'I interviewed him and I didn't get that vibe from him. However, I'm openminded.'

'We should get in touch with Hamilton and ask him where his friend is.'

Kim took her phone out. Dialled a number. 'Ed? It's Kim Smith. Do you know where your friend Stumpy is?'

'He's here with me. Why?'

'We just need to speak with him. Where are you exactly?'

'We're just going into my house. In Trinity.'

'Make sure you stay there, Mr Hamilton. We'll be down there shortly.'

'Okay, we'll be...'

Silence for a moment. Then shouting and a sense of panic.

'Oh my God, no, no, Vicky! Oh God, no!'

'Podge, what's going on?' Kim said, using the man's nickname. But there was no reply. And the phone went dead.

'Frank, Hamilton's in trouble. He's at his house with Wilson. We need to go. I know where he lives.'

FORTY-NINE

It was much colder now that the darkness was holding the city hostage. It didn't feel like Christmas Eve to Miller. He envied the people who were finishing their work for a few days, going to parties and spending time with their friends. Unlike him, who was chasing a killer.

They were in the heart of Trinity now, in a small, modern development called East Lillypot. Named after a house that used to be across the other side of Clark Road, it was sometimes mistakenly referred to as *Lilliput.* Just to confuse taxi drivers and delivery drivers alike.

When Miller pulled the car up to the entrance of the small, dead-end street, a patrol car was blocking his way.

'What's going on here?' he said, rolling down his window.

'Just an incident, sir. Do you live here?'

'Miller. MIT,' he said, showing his warrant card.

The uniform looked embarrassed for a moment, then he saw the blue flashing lights approaching.

'Number nineteen, sir. The ambulance is there as well.' He turned and waved to his partner, who moved the car out of Miller's way, and the convoy of police cars shot into the street and parked near the ambulance, but not blocking it.

He and Kim rushed into the house.

Mickey Wilson, AKA Stumpy, was standing back from the figure who was lying on the living room floor as paramedics attended to her. Uniforms were making sure he didn't leave. Kim went over to the prone figure, telling the paramedics she was a doctor.

'What's going on here?' Miller asked a burly sergeant.

The uniform took him into the hallway. 'It's a bad one, sir. We got a call to come here as an ambulance had been called for a stabbing. We got here just as the paramedics arrived so we came in first to see what was going on. We saw this man on his knees on the floor, applying pressure with a towel.'

Miller looked again and recognised Vicky lying on the carpet. 'Is she going to be okay?'

'They think so. It's a bad wound, but the assailant left before the two men got here.'

'Where's the other one?' *Hamilton.*

'There was only one here. We swept the whole house. Come and see what we found upstairs.'

He led the way and Miller followed.

A uniform was standing guard at one of the bedroom doors while other uniforms were searching the other rooms. Miller nodded to him and stepped past.

The bedroom light was on. The glare from the light bulb reflected off the plastic-covered bodies lying on the bed.

'It looks like they were murdered somewhere else and brought here.' The sergeant looked at Miller. 'There's no sign of any fluids or blood.'

Miller looked at him. 'Did you find anything else?'

'Nothing. We're still looking, but we'll go over the whole place.'

Miller went back downstairs. Vicky was wearing an oxygen mask, and being loaded onto a wheeled stretcher.

'I'll go to the Royal with her,' Kim said.

'Call me when you get more details on her condition.'

She didn't smile as she nodded. Just followed the paramedics out to the waiting ambulance.

'He tried to fucking kill her,' Stumpy said, about to walk towards Miller until a uniform put a hand on his chest.

'Who did? Hamilton?'

Stumpy made a face as if a bad smell had just come

into the room. 'No, of course not. Podge wouldn't hurt Vicky. He's smitten with her.'

'It happens. Love turns sour and there's a fight, and the next thing you know, a knife's being stuck into somebody. I've seen it many times.'

'Listen to yourself. Podge didn't do this, and I know that for a fact, because I was with him when we came in here and found Vicky like that.'

'What about them upstairs?'

'Who?'

Miller had many hours experience of interviewing people and he was getting a feeling about this man standing before him.

'The guests in the bedroom.'

'What guests? What are you talking about? Podge and me have been staying with Vicky at her sister's house. This is Podge's house. Nobody's been staying here.'

Miller could see the genuine confusion on the man's face, which meant one of several things; he was mentally unbalanced and couldn't remember the bodies upstairs; he was a good actor, or he just didn't know about them and was telling the truth.

'Tell me what happened here.'

'Podge – Hamilton – figured that if Vicky was taken in a van, then she could have been brought here. Somebody's out to get him. First they killed his ex-wife, and now they've tried to kill his girlfriend.'

'Maybe he *did* kill his ex-wife. Maybe he has you

believing he's innocent when in fact he's a raving psychopath.'

'No, I don't believe that. We came down in my van together. When we got here, Vicky had already been stabbed.'

'Did she say anything to you when you got here?' He was expecting a negative answer, but was surprised by what he said instead.

'Yes. She was almost losing consciousness, but she said, *Gina*. I'd already called an ambulance and I thought Podge would have stayed but when he heard that name, he was out of here.'

'And you don't know who *Gina* is?' Miller asked, feeling his heart beating faster.

'Never heard of her before. I don't know where Podge has gone, but he's my pal, and if he's in trouble, I need to find him.'

'Don't worry, Mr Wilson, I know who Gina is.' He turned to the uniform. 'Take him to the station at High Street and have him wait in an interview room. Make sure he's not left alone.'

Stumpy was taken away.

'Did somebody call this in?'

'The sergeant did, sir. Forensics are on their way, and more MIT as well.'

As if on cue, Andy Watt walked through the front door, followed by Jimmy Gilmour and Paddy Gibb.

'God rest me weary soul, I was just on me way home when this was called in.'

'That would be me, sir,' the sergeant said.

'So, show me what presents Santa's left for us.'

'Sir, I need to go and check out a lead,' Miller said.

'Don't let me stop you, Frank. I'm past running, so feel free. Take Andy here with you. Keep him out from under me feet.'

'Are you dressing up as Santa or Scrooge for the kids?' Watt said to Gibb.

'Talking of getting the sack...'

'Let's go, Andy. We need to find a woman.'

'Don't let Kim hear you talk like that.'

FIFTY

I lie under the covers, sweating profusely. Gina has a habit of draping a red chiffon scarf over the bedside lamp. It gives the room ambience she once said. Makes it look like a fucking brothel I think. I keep the opinion to myself because this is her flat.

Gina sits up, smiling. 'I like it when our sex is spontaneous,' she says.

I smile at her. 'Me too.'

She stands up, the covers slipping from her naked body. She has a coating of perspiration gleaming on her skin. I take in the curves, her breasts, and her trim stomach. I feel my desire returning, but know she won't be up for round two.

'Where are we going tonight?' I ask, taking a towel out of a drawer.

'I told you, it's a surprise.'

'I love surprises.' I smile again, hoping she's picked

somewhere nice. This dinner is on her, so it should be worth waiting for. She's the one with the money after all.

I watch her walk away to the en suite bathroom. I get up and take my towel in there.

'Mind if I join you?' *I say as the steam rises up to the extractor fan.*

'No funny games. We're going out, remember?'

'I promise.' *Oh well, it was worth a try.*

Ten minutes later, we're both dressing and Gina is putting on the final touches. Then we leave for dinner.

George Street in the middle of Edinburgh is in full swing as revellers go from pub to pub, celebrating Christmas. Gina bemuses me as we stand outside Humphries. It closed early like many businesses.

'Did you forget something,' *I ask her.*

She laughs. 'No, of course not, silly.' *She takes her keys out and opens the doors.*

'You're not thinking of robbing the place, are you?' *I'm smiling when I say it but this is not a reflection of how I'm feeling inside.*

'I have a surprise for you.'

We walk inside.

'Come on upstairs,' *Gina says, switching on the lights, so we can see our way up.*

On the top floor, a table has been set. A quality tablecloth covers the table, and a candlestick sits in the middle. Eight chairs are at the table, four on each side.

'What's this?' I ask, getting a worried feeling in my stomach.

Gina takes out a lighter and lights the candle. 'I wanted to make the atmosphere perfect for tonight.' She smiles at me. 'I want this to be special.'

'It's always special when we're together.'

She beams a smile, one of those, Aren't I a clever girl? kind of smiles. What the fuck has she done?

'I'm debuting the new collection tonight. Just a special preview before the official launch. We have guests coming round in an hour, so I need you to help me get it ready. Just to put up the new banner. I'm having caterers bring food in—'

'Wait, wait,' I say, holding up a hand. 'I thought you and I were just going to have a quiet Christmas?'

'Plenty of time for that when we're old.'

'You didn't tell me about this. Aren't there usually dozens of guests invited to these parties? I mean... Christmas Eve. What were you thinking?' What were you thinking, indeed! My plans are all going to fuck right before my eyes.

'I've been keeping something from you. Something we need to celebrate,' she says, unfazed by my sudden negativity.

Not a child, I think. Please don't let her be pregnant. 'What?'

'I'm opening a store in Manhattan. I've been working behind the scenes for months now, and then I'm going over in the first week of January. It's on Fifth

Avenue, but worth every penny. It's going to make a mint in the first year alone, and then the sky's the limit. What do you think?'

I think I'd better get a fucking move on if some of her twat friends are coming round here. My original plan was to kill her after the New Year, but Christmas Eve is as good a time as any.

'I think I'm done with you being a burden to me.'

The smile drops from her face as if I've slapped her. 'What do you mean?' The flash of lightning in her eyes, her brain sitting at the crossroads, foot on the throttle, ready to fly. The only choice now, which road to take? Disbelief or rip my nuts off?

'Bad choice of words. I know I'm the burden; I can't afford my rent, they're taking my car back and I bought expensive watches with a credit card I can't afford the repayments on.'

Confusion. The engine revving, but first gear hasn't been engaged. 'What are you talking about?'

'It was you who suggested we keep our own places after we got married. I was almost broke and suggested to you we move in to your place, but nobody knew we married in Vegas and your mother died just as we were about to announce it. Let us grieve first, you said. Your uncles and aunts would disapprove. Fuck 'em, I say, but I went along with your plan.'

'Why are you being like this?'

'Why do you think? You're a means to an end, and

202

that end is tonight. You were always going to end up like your mother and the others.'

'My... my mother?'

'I tripped her at the top of the stairs. She went down well, and I figured at her age, she might have broken a hip, but no, she did me proud and broke her neck.'

Her mouth has opened now, the anger that had flashed in her eyes only moments ago replaced with shock. She can't take my words in, her thought process all jumbled and confused.

She steps back. *'What are you talking about? What others?'*

'That thieving fucker who robbed the store and took the earrings? I taught her a lesson.'

'You... you murdered that girl?'

'Of course I did. I get girls from the shelter and I fuck them like it's going out of fashion.'

'You bastard. I'll make sure they put you away for this!'

'Only if I get caught. But this will look like an accident. You've had a little too much to drink, start clowning about and over you go.' I look over the railings into the ground floor showroom.

'You're sick. And to think I let you touch me.'

I laugh at her. *'You're right, I am sick. The wheels in my head don't turn right because they're broken. If I get caught, I'll be put away in a nice little room on my own, with a window that's high up on the wall so I can't climb through it, but that's alright, because I know you* won't be heating up somebody else's bed. But I won't get caught. I'm too smart for that.'

'You're a maniac. I can't believe I married you.'

'Well, you won't have to worry about that in a few minutes. Can you imagine the headline in the Caledonian? "Brilliant Edinburgh designer falls to her death in her store".'

'Get away from me, you fucking freak!' She screams at the top of her lungs.

'It'll be quick. Over the banister and down to your death.'

'Why are you fucking doing this?' she shrieks.

'Money of course,' I tell her. 'I'll inherit everything you have and I won't have to worry about a thing. And the New York property too. Sounds good to me.'

I rush at her and she screams again.

Then I hear the front door opening down below. Somebody else is coming in. Voices. Coming up the stairs.

They arrive on our level. Gina looks confused and relieved all at once.

'He's trying to kill me' Gina says, to the person in front.

I see who's standing behind him. 'What are you doing here?' I grit my teeth and look him in the eye, thinking how much I'm going to enjoy killing them all.

He looks back at me. 'It's over,' he says.

Then I make my move.

FIFTY-ONE

The drive along to the New Town took almost ten minutes with the blue lights going behind the grille of the car and the siren blasting. Miller had a patrol car ahead of him, cutting through the traffic.

They approached George Street by going up Hanover Street and along the one-way system, sirens and lights off when they got close. The windows to the store overlooked the main street and they didn't want to give their quarry a heads-up.

Two more patrol cars pulled into the kerb farther along the street. Miller and Watt got out of their car followed by the uniforms. He tried the door, about to get one of the uniforms to smash it in, but it was open.

There were lights on upstairs, the ground floor in semi-darkness, the light from the Christmas lights and streetlights seeping through the plate glass windows.

Miller sensed the uniforms rushing in behind him.

'Down there, sir,' Watt said, pointing over the banister to the basement level. They could make out the still form of a man, lying face down, blood seeping from his cracked head.

They heard shouting from upstairs and Miller told the uniforms to go and check out the body and call an ambulance.

They made their way up to the next level, where a woman was sitting on the floor, curled up in the corner. Two men were fighting. Not saying anything, but grunting as they grappled, as if one of them was trying to throw the other over the side, to join the corpse below.

Then one of them got the upper hand. He turned to see Miller rushing at him.

Uniforms grabbed hold of him and took him away from the other man who was lying gasping, as if he'd been choked.

The man who the uniforms had hold of looked at Miller and Miller stared him right in the eye.

'Ed Hamilton, I'm arresting you for the murder of Sabrina Hailes and Cindy Stevenson.' *And whoever it is that's lying down there, but we'll get to that later.*

The woman looked over at Miller as he handcuffed Hamilton, and this seemed to knock her out of her catatonic state.

'No! You can't do that!'

Two uniforms stood in between her and Miller, should she think about having a go.

Miller recognised her. It was Gina Rosales, just as he'd suspected it would be. 'I can, Miss Rosales.'

She got to her feet and tried to step forward but was restrained. 'You don't understand; it wasn't Ed. It was that bastard!'

The other man pushed past the uniforms, but Andy Watt stopped him. He punched Watt on the side of the face, but Andy had his extendable baton out and smacked the man on the side of the knee, putting him down.

Uniforms rushed the man and subdued him.

'This is your lucky night, mate,' Watt said. 'You know that song, *All I want for Christmas is my two front teeth?* That was almost you.'

'Get them both away to the station. We'll talk to them up there. Hamilton's friend is already there,' Miller said.

'Stumpy? He's done nothing!' Hamilton said.

'We'll determine that.'

As the two men were marched away in handcuffs, Miller turned to Gina Rosales.

'Now do you want to tell me who's lying on the floor down there?'

FIFTY-TWO

Miller came back into the room with a coffee for himself and Purcell. Sat down with the cups. He didn't think for one minute that the prisoner would pick one up and throw the hot contents at them.

Something told the man it would be the last thing he did on earth if he tried.

The prisoner looked at the clock on the wall. One fifteen am. Christmas Day.

'You can still have a lawyer,' Purcell said. 'In fact, I highly recommend it.'

'No need. And I'll refuse to talk if one sets foot in here.'

The two detectives knew the man would keep up the insanity defence. He'd told them in the car, when he wasn't being recorded. He would be assigned a lawyer whether he wanted one or not.

Miller took the pad from him and handed it over to

Purcell who read the confession first and then gave it back to Miller. He read it and looked the man in the eyes.

'Sign it.'

The man took the pad back and smiled at Miller as he picked up the pen.

Cecil Cavendish.

Miller and Purcell witnessed it, adding their signatures to the bottom of the last page.

There was a knock on the interview room door and a uniform came in with a sheet and handed it to Purcell before leaving.

Purcell read it and showed it to Miller before addressing Cavendish. 'Brian Hall died on the operating table an hour ago. That's another murder charge the PF is going to hit you with.' The man had been lying in the lower level of the store, barely clinging to life, when the paramedics got there.

Cavendish laughed. 'Like I care.'

'Stand up,' Miller said. Cavendish did as he was told. The cameras were still rolling. Miller handcuffed the prisoner's hands and two uniforms took him away to the holding cells downstairs.

Purcell switched the recorders off. 'Well, this has been the most exciting Christmas I've had in a while.'

'You need to get out more, Percy.'

'Tell me about it.' They walked upstairs to the conference room where Ed Hamilton and Gina Rosales were waiting.

They were drinking coffee when Miller and Purcell walked in. A uniform was standing guard just inside.

'So, how are you two holding up?'

'I thought I was toast when you arrested me,' Hamilton said.

Miller and Purcell sat down at the large table. 'Yeah, sorry about that, but everything was pointing to you. Your friend told us how you went charging out after Gina.'

'How's Vicky?'

'The last I heard, she was out of surgery and doing well. Brian Hall died on the table.'

'I'm still trying to get my head round all of this.'

'I know you've made statements, both of you,' Purcell said, 'but give us the story again.'

Gina took a deep breath and let it out slowly before starting. 'Ed's my half-brother. Our mother died a couple of months ago. She had him when she was a young woman, and couldn't look after him, so she put him up for adoption. She went on to be a jewellery designer like myself. She met my father; they got married and had me, a few years after she'd had Ed. I never knew about him until recently, when my mother was dying, and told me.

'So, my parents started *Humphries the Jewellers*, named after my paternal grandmother's maiden name. Ed has the name Hamilton because that was our mother's maiden name. She left the business to both of us.

I've been trying to convince Ed to join the business, as I'm – we're – opening a store in Manhattan. He can run the Edinburgh office.' She smiled at Hamilton, but then her face fell. 'I wanted Cecil to stay here and show Ed the ropes.'

'I've been an office worker all my life. I wouldn't know where to begin,' Hamilton said.

'You would have been taught everything there is to know about the business. You own half of it now, Ed. We have the potential to go far.'

'Let me think about it. It's been such a shock, finding out I have a sister.'

'You've been through a lot, Mr Hamilton,' Miller said.

'Although I didn't like my ex, I wouldn't have harmed her in any way. I even left the house to her and helped her pay it off. She sold it for a good profit and bought the cheaper house in Warriston.'

Gina looked at Miller. 'It seems my manager, Cecil, planned all along to seduce me so he could become my husband, then kill me so he could live the high life on my money. When he found out about Ed, he had to get rid of him too. I can't believe I've been such a fool not to have seen right through him.'

'He was a very convincing liar,' Purcell said.

'You didn't tell me you were married to Cavendish when I asked you if you knew him well,' Miller said.

'I'm sorry about that. It was still a secret then.' She

looked forlorn. 'Was it true, what he said about getting girls from the shelter and using them for sex?'

Miller nodded. 'Yes. Brian got talking to them and offered them a room in an upscale apartment, and then when he took them home, introduced them to his cousin, Cavendish, who charmed them. He would use them and then dump them.'

'And he murdered them?'

'Not all of them. He murdered Sabrina Hailes because he asked her to leave, and to get him back she robbed the store. She called Brian, telling him she needed a favour. Brian was watching Ed's movements as he was infatuated with Vicky and knew Vicky hung around with Hamilton. He told Sabrina where to meet him, as he didn't want to abandon his surveillance of Ed. The timing was all wrong. Sabrina had just turned the store over, and she banged the van door into Ed, and Ed saw Brian.'

'What about the other bodies you told me about earlier? In Ed's house?'

Purcell took a sip of his coffee before answering. 'Many of those teenagers run away because they're in trouble, or because they cause a lot of trouble and their families kick them out. Brian brought a girl home who decided to rip people off. She was a thief back in London. Cavendish killed her and her boyfriend, who had come up to Edinburgh to help his girlfriend.'

Miller looked at her. 'He had spy cameras with audio and one of the forensics team had a look and they saw him killing the girl and her boyfriend. They also found the bit where he killed Sabrina Hailes. He took her out in a trunk he'd added wheels to. Although there are no security cameras in the parking garage under his building, we assume Cavendish put her in the van and drove it away to dump her. Same with the other two. He took them out one at a time.'

'So he was trying to frame me?' Hamilton said.

'Yes. He was trying to make it look as if you killed your ex-wife and then killed the girl and her boyfriend. We found your fingerprint in Vicky's flat, but that's an easy thing to do, if you know how. He could have lifted your print off something on a piece of tape and then put the tape onto the cistern handle.'

'He was that desperate to get me out of the picture?'

'He wanted Gina to have all the money. Cavendish was actually very talkative. He said he was in debt up to his ears. His rent is overdue, his Porsche is being repossessed, and he's living from month to month. By marrying Gina, all his money worries would be over. He could have kept going for another six months on his own, and then he would be in the crapper, but by then he thought you would have been found dead somewhere and he'd inherit the lot.'

'Did Brian help him?'

Miller shook his head. 'No, he was an unwitting pawn in all of this. All he did was bring the girls home. He didn't realise his cousin was a killer. He needed somewhere to stay and liked Cavendish's apartment, so he got the girls. Brian was also in a young offenders institution when he was a teenager. Cavendish said it was he himself who tried to rape the neighbour's daughter, but Brian took the fall for it because he was a juvenile.'

'I thought he was at the store to help Cavendish when I arrived, but he was there to stop him. He said Cavendish told him he'd got rid of the girl he'd just taken in and her boyfriend. Hall didn't want any part of it and knew he had to contact the police but he couldn't prove any of it,' said Miller.

'So what happens now?' Hamilton asked.

'He'll be remanded in custody until his first court appearance, which will be in a couple of days, and his lawyer will go for the diminished responsibility plea.'

'Broken wheels,' Gina said.

'What?' Miller looked at her.

'That's what he said to me before you arrived. The wheels in his mind are broken, so he's not responsible.'

'I think a jury will see through that.'

'Right,' Purcell said, 'time to go home. We've had somebody take a statement from your friend Wilson, and he's waiting downstairs. We'll make sure you all get home. There's a car waiting to drive you.'

They all stood and left the room.

'You're coming round to our place for Christmas dinner,' Miller said to Purcell.

'Thanks, but I couldn't. It's a time for family. I'll be fine at the hotel.'

'It wasn't a request. Kim invited you. If you don't turn up, I'll get the blame. Four o'clock. Don't be late.'

'I won't argue with Kim.'

'Ed, I'll catch up with you,' Gina said. 'I want a word with Inspector Miller first.'

'I'll have this officer take you down to the back door where the car's waiting,' Purcell said, walking away with Hamilton and the uniform.

When they were alone in the corridor, Gina looked at Miller. 'Can I ask, do you have anybody special in your life?'

'My girlfriend. And her daughter. We live together. Why do you ask?'

'If you're thinking of popping the question, come into the store. I'll make sure you're taken care of.'

'Way ahead of you,' he replied, taking a small box out of his pocket. 'I've been carrying this about all day.' He opened it up and showed it to her.

Gina smiled. 'It's beautiful. I designed that one myself. She'll love it.'

'I know. I wanted to make it special.'

'Let me know how it goes. And thank you for everything, Frank.'

'Come on, I'll walk you down to the car. It's been a long day and I've a little girl at home who will be up early wanting to play with all her new toys. But first, I need to go and wake up my girlfriend's father and ask his permission to marry his daughter.'

'Do you think your girlfriend will have a jumper for you for Christmas?'

'Count on it.

ABOUT THE AUTHOR

John Carson is originally from Edinburgh, Scotland, but now lives in New York State with his wife and family. And two dogs. And four cats.

website - johncarsonauthor.com
 Facebook - JohnCarsonAuthor
 Twitter - JohnCarsonBooks
 Instagram - JohnCarsonAuthor

Printed in Great Britain
by Amazon